DEATH IN FLAMES

Death in Flames

A Patrick Dawlish Mystery

**John Creasey *writing as*
Gordon Ashe**

Copyright © 1943 by John Creasey

ISBN: 978-1-5040-9822-9

This edition published in 2025 by Open Road Integrated Media, Inc.
180 Maiden Lane
New York, NY 10038
www.openroadmedia.com

DEATH IN FLAMES

CHAPTER ONE

FLOWERS FOR CAPTAIN DAWLISH

'*Captain Dawlish, please, Captain Dawlish!*'

The piping treble of a page-boy's voice echoed about the sacrosanct quiet of the smoking-room at the Carilon, causing many somnolent members to open their eyes; with disapproval in some cases, and in others, a faint curiosity. 'Captain Dawlish, please. Captain *Dawlish!*'

Walking swiftly, glancing to right and left, the page-boy sped on. The carpet deadened all sound of his movement, but the slight breeze created by his hurrying stirred the royal heads of a dozen arum lilies, rising in stately fashion from the florist's basket he was carrying.

'Captain Dawlish, please, Captain *Dawlish!*'

''Pon my soul,' rumbled ffoliot-Green. 'What will happen next? What on earth does Dawlish want with those? Eh?' He glared at Colonel Pomfret, opposite him; both were red-faced and white-haired, both roused from the middle of an afternoon nap.

'No idea,' said Pomfret irritably. 'Confounded fellow is always creating a disturbance of some kind. Saw him at luncheon. Humph, arum lilies, absurd.'

Along the wide, marble corridors of the Carilon the page-boy hastened, calling monotonously for Dawlish. Near the billiard-room a waitress approached him carrying a tray with several tankards. At sight of the boy she nodded towards the billiard-room. She had been at the Carilon for only a short time, but there were a few members whom she knew well, and Captain Dawlish was one of them.

The boy strode on, and at the door of the billiard-room his piping treble smote the ears of three men inside. 'Captain Dawlish, *please!*'

Standing by one of the six tables, only two of which were occupied, was a tall, broad-shouldered man with crisp fair hair, a formidable chin and a broken nose. His eyes were blue-grey, and as they turned towards the door they held a smile. About the giant, and thus he could be justly called, was an indefinable air of good humour; he was a man whom most people instinctively liked.

Near him, bending over the billiard-table and about to attempt a red loser, was a man nearly as tall, but dark and thin. He struck the cue-ball, which hesitated near the pocket and then dropped in.

'Twenty-seven,' said Dawlish, 'and you nearly missed it. Wait a moment, someone's bringing me a present.'

The dark man looked round at the page-boy. The solitary man at the other table, who had been industriously potting the red in a game of snooker with himself, did the same. Both watched the boy's approach to Dawlish.

'Just left for you, sir.'

Dawlish eyed the lilies contemplatively, tipped the boy and then asked: 'Was there any message?'

'There's a note in the baskit, sir, thank you, sir.' The boy saluted smartly, then turned and hurried off.

Neil Cousins, the game forgotten, and Andy Cunningham,

who had been the odd man out, looked on as Dawlish extracted an envelope from the basket, and slit it open.

'Who the dickens sent you those?' demanded Neil curiously. 'It isn't St Valentine's Day—or is it?' As Andy shook his head, the other went on: 'It's obvious that he's been breaking more hearts, what would Felicity say?'

'Be quiet, oafs,' said Dawlish, smoothing the note out. As he read, his brows contracted, and the good-humour faded from his eyes. The change was noticeable, and affected the others to a lesser degree. The room was very silent for some seconds, and then Dawlish handed the note to Neil. Cunningham read it over the other's shoulder.

'I could not help thinking of you, Captain Dawlish, when I saw these. So fortunate that they are not yet made into a wreath, don't you think?'

There was no address, and no signature. The envelope was type-written, bearing only Dawlish's name.

The silence lengthened, until Cousins broke it with an impatient:

'What in Hades is that about?'

'More to the point is what in Hades has Pat been up to!' said Cunningham gently. 'Arum lilies for a funeral. If it were anyone else I'd say it was a rather unpleasant practical joke, but—'

'It must be a joke,' protested Cousins.

'Does Pat think so?' demanded Cunningham. 'Out with it Pat, what's doing?'

Dawlish quietly replaced the letter in the envelope, and tucked it into his pocket. He raised the basket and eyed the flowers thoughtfully, then placed them on a chair.

'Not a bad effort, is it?'

'No side-tracking from you,' declared Cunningham. 'What's it all about?'

'I'm not sure that you ought to know,' said Dawlish slowly. 'I'm not really sure that I know myself, but—' he shrugged. 'I could tell you a story. Let's finish the game, and then—'

'The game's finished,' declared Neil Cousins decisively.

They strolled to the far end of the room, ensconced themselves in comfortable chairs and then waited in expectancy while the large man considered his words.

He was not at ease, and the others were aware of it, holding that basket of lilies had affected him more than might have been expected. They did not know that he was wondering whether to put them off with a plausible story that would satisfy their curiosity but arouse no speculation. Yet he realized that he had already shown them that he was concerned by the flowers, and they were not men likely to be easily deceived.

Before he spoke, many things passed through his mind.

When in a mood for discussing the past, he would often declare that he had a Jekyll-and-Hyde complex; and there were many who agreed with him, including Superintendent William Trivett of Scotland Yard, the Assistant Commissioner, and also Felicity Deverall, to whom Dawlish was engaged. For the most part he was a genial man, a man-about-town in the days of peace, and a soldier, in time of war, who resented the fact that he was always stationed in England. There were many who believed that in peace-time his life was wasted, and that he could be justly blamed for doing nothing useful. Trivett had once subscribed to that opinion, but seven times in the past three years there had been an affair of some consequence occupying the urgent attention of the police, an affair in which Dawlish had been involved. Sometimes he appeared to be drawn unwillingly into the mesh of investigation, sometimes without the approval of the authorities. Latterly the authorities had not only approved, but requested his co-operation.

Trivett had once been heard to say:

'When he gets an idea into his head he just rides it, and cuts out everything else. If he were a policeman he'd be reprimanded a dozen times in a couple of days; he doesn't care a damn about regulations. But—' and here Trivett had raised his hands helplessly and added: 'He gets there. I don't know how, and I don't think he does. But he gets there.'

Of these things both Cunningham and Cousins knew little, but it happened that although they were old friends of Dawlish they had been abroad, or otherwise occupied, at the times of the earlier affairs. They had heard of them and marvelled, although they had been told little by Dawlish himself. Yet they accepted what they had heard without question.

Sitting in the billiard-room of the Carilon, in sight of the basket of arum lilies, Dawlish smiled a little before he said:

'I suppose you'd better know the truth of it.'

'There'll be trouble if we don't,' said Cunningham. 'Who sent the *in memoriam* offering, for a start?'

'I don't know,' said Dawlish, 'but if all goes well we'll find out.' He frowned. 'I'm not sure that we oughtn't to start finding out before I tell you any part of the story.'

'You don't move from here until you've talked,' said Cousins firmly. 'Out with it.'

Dawlish shrugged.

'Please yourselves, but remember you asked for it. The arum lilies would seem to be connected to a little French girl frightened out of her life.'

'Ah-ah,' said Cunningham. 'So there is a feminine angle?'

'The little French girl came to me the other day,' continued

Dawlish, 'and told me that she was frightened, and asked whether I could help her. She had a deep-seated dislike of approaching the police, but Felicity and I reasoned with her, and at last she consented to tell them all about it. A charming little creature,' he added thoughtfully, 'not a day more than twenty, but as old as the hills in some ways. The thing I couldn't understand was why she came to me.'

'Do you know now?' asked Cunningham.

'No-o. At least, she said that a friend told her that I might be able to help. She wouldn't give the name of the friend, and spoke with an odd mixture of extreme reticence and an uninhibited frankness. Rather strange, I thought.'

'Are we going to hear what she said, or aren't we?' demanded Cunningham.

'I have already told you what she said,' said Dawlish. 'That she was frightened was clearly apparent. Why she should be so, was not so clear, except that strange men have been following her, and others have been attempting to blackmail her; or so she said. Until this afternoon I wasn't sure whether she was genuine, but someone apparently doesn't like to think that she's appealed to me.' He added with a smile: 'That's the lot, believe it or not. Yvonne Lejeune, a pretty enough name, but one anyone could think up, escaped from Occupied France to Unoccupied, thence to Spain and Portugal, and eventually to England. When she reached here she reported to the authorities in the approved manner. Then she found herself followed, and preferred to see me rather than the police. Odd, I think you'll agree?'

'Ye-es,' said Cunningham, thoughtfully. 'Why did you pass her on to the police?'

Dawlish shrugged.

'Before the war I might have been justified in looking into it myself, but not now. The only thing at stake was Yvonne

Lejeune's opinion of me, and that was neither here nor there. Felicity seemed to convince her though, and she seemed happy enough about seeing the police after we'd finished.' He paused, and then added: 'If the arum lilies *are* connected with Yvonne, we'll find out, and if they *aren't* I can't think of any other show where someone might try to warn me off.'

'Warn you off?' said Cousins slowly.

'Yes, little man,' said Dawlish mockingly. 'The anonymous sender says, as clearly as he can: "Keep off the grass or you'll be buried under it." I think I'll be justified in doing something about that, don't you? And it's come at a time when I've three weeks' leave, so'—he beamed about him—'one way and the other we might be busy. Big things out of little things grow, I once learned in Form I. It could even be interesting.'

'Where do we start?' demanded Cunningham simply.

'You really want to be in it?'

'Don't be an ass,' protested Cousins. 'We *are* in it.'

Dawlish carrying the lilies, they made their way through the Club, avoiding the more crowded rooms. Inquiries at the desk elucidated the facts that the flowers had been delivered just as Dawlish had received them. A red-haired boy had brought them. There was no indication of where the flowers had been bought, nor for whom the youth worked.

'So we're completely in the dark,' mused Dawlish as they stepped into the warm spring sunlight. 'We could ask every flower shop in London whether they've sold twelve arum lilies to a suspicious looking individual, but it wouldn't do a lot of good, and take up a lot of time.'

'I was wondering where to begin,' admitted Cunningham. 'But there doesn't seem much we can do.'

'What appalling pessimism,' exclaimed Dawlish with mock astonishment. 'Here's something for a start. We take a taxi to the Yard, and tell Trivett all about it. The police find out who supplied the lilies, which information Trivett, being a good soul, passes on to me. The art of this business,' he added with a grin, 'is knowing how much to get the others to do for you.'

'I thought we were going to handle it ourselves,' grumbled Cousins. 'Anyone could go to the police.'

'Of course they could,' said Dawlish cheerfully. 'And anyone could assume that they will be allowed to get that far unseen. Others might think that they would be watched. Did that occur to either of you?' he asked gently. 'Don't look round, but when we've started, keep your eyes open, particularly for a red-headed youth. All right?'

He hailed a taxi. As they waited for its approach, a red-haired youth, lying on the grass of the park, sat up and watched them.

CHAPTER TWO

NOT A BAD IDEA

'Lilies,' quoth Patrick Dawlish to Superintendent Trivett. 'Fairest of flowers but demanding the most careful handling, Bill. You'll look after that, won't you?'

The basket of lilies was standing on Trivett's desk in the latter's room at Scotland Yard. Trivett, a tall, good-looking man with a dark moustache and disconcertingly direct grey eyes, nodded enigmatically. There was just room for three chairs in front of his desk, and the three men were occupying them.

'Just what do you mean by that?' he asked.

'We-ell,' said Dawlish judiciously, 'I don't know much about flowers, but I do know that lilies are out of season at the moment. Also, they're packed very carefully. I did rather wonder what would happen when one was taken out. I mean, supposing it was intended to give me a shock?'

Trivett frowned a little.

'You haven't touched them?'

'Certainly not,' said Dawlish severely.

'Did you bring those things all the way here thinking that the basket might explode?' gasped Cousins.

'Why not?' demanded Dawlish. 'It would be a pretty plan, assuming that someone doesn't want me around any longer, and I can't imagine why that should be. Eh, Bill?'

'If you've told us everything about the Lejeune girl, I can't,' conceded Trivett.

'Well, you know all that I know. Yvonne is the only one who might be able to explain more, and we've not reached any certain decision about that.'

Cousins said curiously:

'What are you going to do with the lilies?'

'Leave 'em with Trivett,' said Dawlish promptly. 'Any objections, Bill?'

'I'll have them examined,' Trivett promised him. 'Is that the only reason you came here?'

'The one and only,' said Dawlish, 'but while I'm here you might open up about Yvonne. Has she given you any more information?'

'Nothing at all,' Trivett assured him. 'She's reporting to Great Marlborough Street every day, as arranged, and she's being watched. No one appears to have followed her.' He frowned, and then added thoughtfully: 'I wonder why she came to you, Pat? It can't be a hoax just for the sake of it, but there doesn't seem to be any reason in it.'

'Well,' said Dawlish, 'if we accept her first story on its face value, she believed that she was being followed. She came to see me, and then you. The following stopped, implying that whoever was interested in her didn't want to be discovered. And yet the same someone chooses to make himself noticed now,' continued Dawlish very thoughtfully. 'Odd, Bill, but I suppose we'd better leave it at that for the moment.'

'Right.' Trivett stood up. 'Let me know if anything else happens.'

Five minutes later they were ushered out of the portals of Scotland Yard. As they gained the pavement Cousins turned to regard Dawlish with something akin to impatience.

'What the dickens was the use of that?' he demanded. 'You didn't say a word about the red-haired beggar—and you knew darned well that he followed us all the way. He might be around still,' added the dark man with feeling. 'What was the point of talking all that drip about baskets blowing up?'

'Trivett would be justly annoyed if I concealed pertinent ideas,' said Dawlish reproachfully, 'and just in case there's anything lethal about the basket, it wouldn't be fair to make him take chances. He might not have thought of it for himself, you see. As for what we've done, we've established the fact that we went straight to the police with the flowers. Red-head watched us, and will of course report. It should successfully convey the idea that I am not having anything to do with the show myself, but leaving it to the police.'

'But you said—' began Cunningham.

'Think, man, think!' said Dawlish impatiently. 'Trivett will tell you that the first essential in this particular form of warfare is to make the other side believe that it knows what's in your mind, and red-head must surely think that I've washed my hands of the affair. Savvy?'

'Of course I do,' said Cousins a trifle heatedly, 'and also the fact that we'll see no more of him, and the whole affair, as far as we're concerned, is probably washed up.'

'In which case we'll have a quiet leave, and enjoy ourselves,' said Dawlish. 'But somehow I don't think it's likely.'

'And I don't think you're normal,' said Cousins coldly.

'But—I thought everyone had already agreed on that,' said Dawlish with evident satisfaction. 'Let's get to the flat and tell Felicity all about it.'

They walked towards Audeley Street, where he had a small flat, in which Felicity and a friend were staying. Cunningham and Cousins lived nearby, at the London home of Cunningham's family, and thus they were able to keep in constant and easy touch with one another.

They did not hurry, and so far as Dawlish could see no one followed or showed any interest in them. The youthful red-head had disappeared, after following them as far as the gates of Scotland Yard, and his disappearance obviously rankled with Cunningham and Cousins.

To Dawlish, it seemed that the sending of the lilies was either quite senseless, or intended to ensure his interest. He hummed a little to himself, ignoring the bodeful silence of his companions.

Arriving at the flat, he opened the door with his latch-key, stepped inside and stopped abruptly.

Voices greeted them, Felicity Deverall's and one other. As the door widened, Dawlish caught a glimpse of the speaker, and he stopped dead still.

'My oath!' exclaimed Cunningham.

Felicity turned abruptly, but none of them really saw her. All of them were looking at a red-haired youth, whose voice was rising—even squeaking—with prolonged loquacity.

'That's what I say, Miss, and believe me I'm serious, I wouldn't let him do anything more if I were you. It wouldn't be safe for him. I don't mind admitting I'd be in Queer Street if anyone knew that I was talking to you like this, but there're some things where I put my foot down, and this is one of them. Will you talk to him?'

The situation was absurd: the youngster must know that the others were on the threshold, and it was obvious that he meant Dawlish when he said 'him'. But he showed no awareness of their presence, and talked as if they were out of earshot.

'Will you?' he repeated earnestly.

Felicity threw up her hands. 'Thank heavens you've come, Pat.'

For the first time the youngster turned his head.

He showed no surprise at sight of the others.

'I've got to be going,' he said.

Dawlish stood squarely in the doorway, with Cunningham and Cousins on either side of him.

'Why don't you start going now?' asked Dawlish pleasantly.

The youth did not acknowledge the words, but turned on his heel towards the farther door of the room. As he passed her he put out a hand and gripped Felicity's shoulder, spinning her into the three men. For a moment there was confusion which cleared to the sound of the youth's footsteps clattering down the iron steps of the tradesman's staircase.

Dawlish's voice rose sharply:

'Neil, try and catch him at the back.'

He reached the farther door in three long strides, pulled it open and hurried through. By the time he was in the dining-room, Neil Cousins was racing down the front stairs, hoping to reach the alleyway which served the rear of the houses before the red-head disappeared. Dawlish stepped swiftly to the iron landing. He was in time to see the red-haired youth hurrying along the service alley towards Audeley Street. There was just a chance that Cousins would meet him, but none that Dawlish could catch up with him.

Rather shamefacedly he rejoined the others.

'Well, he certainly put one over us that time. I should have known better. Are you all right, Fel?'

He looked into her grey-green eyes, seeing in them a hint of apprehension.

'I suppose I am,' she said with a little laugh, 'he didn't get violent until you arrived.'

Cousins came slumping up the stairs looking ruffled and out of countenance.

'I lost him,' he said disgustedly. 'I caught a glimpse of him tearing off towards Piccadilly, and then some clumsy lout got in my way. There wasn't a chance of catching up. What a nerve the fellow had!'

'H'm, yes,' said Dawlish. 'You mean the clumsy lout as well as the red-head, I don't doubt that you were stopped with malice aforethought. Capable gentry, these.'

'But—' began Cunningham.

'Don't argue with him,' advised Felicity. 'If he thinks the man who knocked against you is one of the crowd, nothing will make him change his mind, not that it matters one way or the other.'

'Squashed utterly and completely,' said Dawlish wryly. 'What did the talkative gentleman have to say to you, darling?'

'I think you heard most of it,' said Felicity reflectively. 'He scared me for a moment, before he started talking, and then, if I hadn't known you, I'd have taken him for a lunatic. He begged me to prevent you from taking any interest in what was happening. It was foolish for me to encourage you in helping another woman, and if you persisted you would only get hurt. He went on and on, and I was wondering if I could get to the telephone, or even shout for the police, when I heard you coming. The amazing thing was that he took no notice at all of you. He must have heard you talking outside, but he just went on and on.'

'A new method of approach,' said Dawlish. He rumpled her hair with a disarming grin, and gave her a brief résumé of what had happened. She made little comment, but appeared to be very thoughtful, retiring within herself as if trying to reason out the motive before discussing it with the others.

Dawlish knew that she was resenting the whole business. In the past she had always felt that sharp animosity towards anyone who encouraged him to take a part in such affairs, although they had met in the course of one of them. She would do nothing to hinder, and in fact much to help: but she hated the thought of further trouble, and refrained from saying so only when it was obvious that comment would do no good.

'And so I took the lilies to Trivett, and the red-head came here instead of going to report,' went on Dawlish. 'I wonder if red-head saw me go to the Yard and decided that the bait wasn't working, so came on here to make reasonably sure that I would be personally affronted and therefore personally involved?'

'But why should anyone try to involve you?' demanded Felicity. 'Is there any sense in it?'

'I haven't seen the sense yet,' admitted Dawlish, 'but there may be some lurking in the background.' He was silent for some seconds, and then added: 'If we assume that red-head and his friends want me involved, do we also assume that Yvonne came with her pretty little story with the same object in mind?'

'Now listen Pat,' began Cunningham, 'there's no need to make it as complicated as all that.'

'Complicated?' echoed Dawlish. 'It's as plain as a pikestaff. We assume in the first place that my attention is wanted—without going into whys and wherefores, or whether it's sensible or not. Granted?'

'Ye-es,' admitted Cunningham.

'Good. First Yvonne comes and tells a story which should be enough to make me take a look at this and that. Instead I persuade her to go to the police. When she first came she was almost hysterical at mention of the police, but when it came down to final issues she told them without hesitating, proving that there was no reason at all why she shouldn't have gone to them in the first place.'

'I see what you mean,' said Cousins slowly. 'Yvonne had a second line of defence if you were adamant about the police, and she used it. But she didn't tell you the full story of why your help was wanted.'

'Something like that,' approved Dawlish amiably. 'Yvonne, acting on the instructions of a gentleman we'll call X, doesn't work the oracle. So they try the lilies. They don't work either, so they try invasion tactics, a personal affront which I surely can't overlook. You can almost see him saying to himself: "This'll get the beggar."'

'But I don't see why,' objected Cousins.

'No one's trying to see why at the moment,' said Dawlish lazily. 'It's hidden in beautiful obscurity. If we go any further it will come to us, and if we don't it doesn't matter. At the moment we've had a nasty set-back, but things aren't too bad. Red-head and his friend X don't know what we're going to do, and Trivett is convinced that I'm being perfectly straightforward.'

'And you're going to be, of course,' said Felicity quickly.

'We-ell, we'll try,' said Dawlish, 'but human nature can be tried, too far. Even if we sit back and do nothing, the chances are that they'll have another shot at us.'

'It's nice of you to include us all,' said Cunningham sweetly. 'And you can't convince me, Pat, that you're as innocent as you pretend to be. You know something else—confound it, you must! They wouldn't try to get your interest just for the sake of it.'

'They must think you can help them, anyhow,' said Cousins quickly.

'Ye-es,' said Dawlish, rubbing his nose. 'Yes, they do.'

'That's precisely what they do think,' said Felicity repressively. 'They know he's on leave, and there's something worrying them. They believe Pat's the man for their money, but they're trying to intrigue him. They know a straightforward approach wouldn't be nearly so alluring. I wonder why you don't put a brass plate on the door. "Private Investigations a Speciality", she added, 'though even that would seem superfluous. I've had half-a-dozen people asking for you in the past three months.'

Dawlish looked at her keenly.

'Is that an exaggeration, or—'

Felicity waved a hand airily. 'Do you expect me to *count* them?'

'Well, it might be a help,' admitted Dawlish. 'Six in the last three months is quite a lot, my sweet. You couldn't by chance remember them?'

'I may have kept the cards,' said Felicity. 'If I have, they're in your writing-case.'

'Praise be for your tidy mind!' exclaimed Dawlish, and made a dive for his bedroom. He returned after a few minutes with a small writing-case. He opened it, and from a pocket extracted some visiting-cards. There were seven in all, and he glanced at them one by one, his eyes narrowing and his lips pursed.

'If we want to look into it, here's the chance.'

'We don't,' said Felicity flatly, 'but you may as well tell us what you've found.'

'A very simple and interesting fact,' said Dawlish prosily. 'Here are seven visitors, all asking for help because they've seen my name in the papers some time or other. Well, that's reasonable enough. But can any of you, by any stretch of the imagination, explain why three of them should come from different people with different names living at the same address—unless they have similar motives?'

CHAPTER THREE

THE BRITTLING HOTEL

They all bent forward to see the three cards bearing the same address, which lay on the palm of Dawlish's hand. One bore the name: Mr Richard Playfair, Dramatic Critic; another: Mr T. H. K. McFee, while the third was inscribed: Miss Phoebe Lancaster, Impersonator. The address of all three was Brittling Hotel, Bayswater Road. Dawlish said plaintively: 'Sweet, can't you remember the remotest detail of what they wanted, or what they looked like?'

Felicity shook her head.

'I can't think of any reason why I should remember,' she said reflectively, 'but I might, if we were to go to the Yard and tell Trivett all about it.'

The three men stared at her, aghast and dismayed.

'Damn it, you can't do that!' protested Cousins warmly. 'We might be able to help these people. I mean, Pat might.'

'Obviously they don't want to go to the police,' put in Cunningham. 'It might do a tremendous amount of harm. I mean, supposing you were in the same position and anyone did that to you, what would you feel about it?'

'Well, let's imagine them,' suggested Dawlish dreamily, 'starting with Mr Richard Playfair. I picture him as a short, oldish man, with grey hair worn like Lloyd George's, a butterfly collar and probably a cravat with a pin. Black coat and striped trousers, of course, and very precise in his manner. Is that anywhere near the mark?'

'No,' said Felicity, 'and I'm not as easy to delude as all that, darling.' For a moment she and Dawlish regarded each other without speaking, and then she went on quietly: 'Pat, are you serious? Wouldn't it be better to let Trivett know?'

'I don't think so,' said Dawlish quietly, 'it looks to me like a well-conceived effort to make me visit them, or locate them, and I just can't imagine anyone with a reason for wishing me harm at the moment. So let's credit them with good motives, for a start.'

'Y'know, I'm in deep waters,' confessed Cousins, eyeing Dawlish with some bewilderment. 'Didn't you give Trivett exactly the converse to work on?'

'He's as crafty as the very devil in a case like this,' said Felicity with feeling. 'Of course he did. He doesn't want Trivett to think that he's seen the other possibility, and no one but Pat would be likely to. At the moment he's wallowing in the thought that Phoebe Lancaster, McFee and Playfair, and probably Yvonne and the nasty little red-haired brat for good measure, are all waiting at the Brittling Hotel hoping desperately that he's going to rescue them from an awful fate. Don Quixote in a British warm, in fact. That's Pat.'

Dawlish shifted, a little uneasily. It was plain to see that Felicity's comments had stung. He knew she felt bitter about his constant—and to her, unnecessary—involvements in danger. On the other hand, when she said that the common-sense thing to do was to take the whole story to Trivett, she was right. He had, however, no intention of doing this; for one thing he believed that if Scotland Yard took the matter up, those involved would immediately go to earth.

There was another factor, too, one which he did not particularly want to emphasize. For nearly twelve months he had been at a desk in Whitehall; until he had first gone there he had not realized the appalling dullness which could encompass an officer in the Intelligence Department, or the almost invariable monotony of intelligence work. Only once had there been a break; and since then he had done little but dictate and sign letters. Now that he had a long spell of leave, he felt it was only his due to seize this opportunity to shake off the boredom of the past few months.

Felicity was looking at him with more understanding than he cared about. She said at last: 'Pat, how much do you want to look into this?'

'No more than I'd like to look into anything which might give me some exercise,' admitted Dawlish, 'and this show is promising, you must admit that.'

Felicity threw up her hands. 'All right. I give in. When are you going to visit the Brittling?'

'Bless your heart!' exclaimed Dawlish. 'Fairly soon, although it might be best to make it after dark. For the moment, how's your memory?'

Felicity had generosity. Having capitulated she would not be half-hearted about it. She sat back with her eyes closed, searching her memory.

'Playfair is tall, thin, old and shabby,' she chanted. 'A deep mellow voice and a charming manner. In fact, the perfect picture of a gentleman in adversity. Does that convey anything?'

'If we ever see him and don't recognize him we deserve to be shot,' admitted Dawlish. 'McFee?'

'Short, fair, Scottish accent—which occasionally slipped,' said

Felicity. 'As for Phoebe Lancaster, I should think she must do male impersonations, and now prefers the part to her own. She wore a skirt, but it was obvious it should have been slacks.'

Cousins grimaced.

'No golden tresses?'

Felicity shook her head. 'Very masculine. But remember I only saw them once apiece, and they might strike me very differently if they came again.'

'When are we going to see 'em?' demanded Cousins.

'That is a point,' admitted Dawlish. 'I said after dark, but—' he glanced at his wrist-watch. 'It's half-past four, that gives us about three hours to black-out.'

'They've waited so long that a few hours won't make any difference,' Felicity pointed out.

'They're getting more pressing,' said Dawlish. 'Let's have some tea, and then we can get along. An outside survey only for a start, I think.'

'In that case, I'm coming,' said Felicity.

Both Cunningham and Cousins offered to help her get the tea, and Dawlish waved them towards the kitchen, while he leaned back in his chair, eyes closed and legs stretched in front of him.

He was trying to picture the three callers as well as Yvonne and the red-headed youth. None of them had done anything which could be labelled as violence. The possibility that the lilies might contain something lethal he dismissed without further thought; he had suggested it as a means to make Trivett believe that he, Dawlish, was going to do nothing about it.

Dawlish's lips curved.

'Here I go again,' he thought. 'One day Bill is going to go off the deep end.' Then, after a sudden outburst of laughter from the kitchen, the telephone rang.

Dawlish heaved himself to his feet, and reached for the receiver. The caller was Trivett, and not in the best of tempers.

'We've had a look at the lilies, Pat. There's nothing wrong with them whatever. Who's been putting ideas into your head?'

'They seem to arrive on their own,' protested Dawlish, with mock innocence. 'Have you discovered where the lilies were bought?'

'Not yet. Do you really think it's worth finding out?'

'We-ell, if you prefer to risk having to buy a black tie and taking half a day off for my funeral, no,' said Dawlish. 'If the Johnny with the pretty taste in *billets doux* is serious, I'd like to know more about him, but I'll leave it to the police. All I want is a quiet life.'

'I think I'd better send Munk to follow you about,' said Trivett darkly. 'When you vaporize sentiments like that it's time to be wary. What are you doing tonight?'

'Staying here, probably,' said Dawlish, and added mendaciously: 'we might go for a stroll, but if you're thinking of coming over—'

'I might look in,' said Trivett. 'Cheerio.'

Dawlish smiled, not without satisfaction, as he replaced the receiver. Had Trivett really suspected that he was thinking of taking a keener interest he would not have said so, but would have sent a man to watch him. And the man would not be Detective-Sergeant Munk, whom Dawlish knew well, but one whom it was possible that Dawlish had never seen before. The idea that Trivett might, in fact, be doing just that, caused Dawlish to step to the window overlooking the street, and watch the passers-by. No one appeared to be lounging, and everyone he saw either turned into a house, or went round one corner or another.

'I think I can take him at his face value,' he mused. 'I wonder what the Brittling's like?'

Over tea, it came to him that Cunningham and Cousins could survey the hotel as well as he could, and over tea suggested it. Both Cunningham and Cousins jumped at the idea. Within ten minutes they were making their way noisily down the stairs, and Felicity was looking at Dawlish, with a glimmer of a smile on her lips.

'You do know how to handle everyone, darling, don't you?' she said dryly.

He grinned, proffering a cup to be refilled. 'It's certainly a queer show, darling, and it might give us a lot to think about. Whoever is behind it has an ingenious mind, we have to grant him that.'

'I suppose they'll be all right,' said Felicity.

'Who? Andy and Neil? Great Scott, they're only going to walk past the place and tell us what it looks like,' said Dawlish, 'we needn't worry about them. Let's forget them for half-an-hour, and talk about—' he chuckled. 'Anything you like.'

They succeeded in forgetting the affair of the arum lilies, Yvonne and the peculiar callers.

There was much to talk about.

Some time before, they had decided that it was wise to defer getting married until after the war, but Dawlish often regretted it. He had anticipated spending a great deal of time overseas, and still lived in the hope that he might do so; only that kept them single. He knew that there was a likelihood that one day they would get tired of the situation, and get married in a rush. The difficulty was that although he was often at the flat for the evenings, and in fact rarely at the office after six o'clock, Felicity, serving in the A.T.C., was often on night duty. It was due to that, that she had seen the callers from the Brittling Hotel.

Meanwhile, Cunningham and Cousins went by taxi to Bayswater Road, instructing the driver to take them slowly past the Brittling Hotel. It was a grey, forbidding house in a long terrace, with a small notice-board outside. At first glance it was depressing.

'Not much of a show,' said Cunningham.

'About the kind of place you'd expect after Felicity's descriptions,' said Cousins.

A hundred yards farther on they dismissed the cabby, and began to stroll back.

Neither of them looked self-conscious, although each admitted to feeling a little out of his depths. Cunningham glanced behind several times, half-expecting to see the red-headed youth, but all the pedestrians appeared to be hurrying to or from the station.

'I wonder if Pat would see more than we do?' asked Cousins. 'D'you know, Andy, I've a queer feeling that there's something of consequence brewing.'

'I share it,' said Cunningham, and then said irritably: 'It's damned silly, of course.'

They were fifty yards from the hotel, when a taxi drew up outside it, and a youth descended, his red hair clearly seen. There was no doubt at all that it was the same youth who had followed them, and had so easily outwitted Dawlish. If they noticed anything strange it was the fact that he hurried from the cab without paying the driver, who started off again immediately.

The door of the hotel opened and then closed sharply.

Cunningham's eyes held a gleam of excitement.

'Whew!! One of us had better get over to the telephone and let Pat know. He'll want—'

He stopped abruptly.

The door of the hotel had opened again. A girl hurried out. She was small, well-dressed and obviously alarmed. She reached the pavement, turned away from Cunningham and Cousins and began to run in the opposite direction. A second woman followed, much taller, and running with the easy stride of a man.

'What the devil's going on?' exclaimed Cunningham.

Both he and Cousins began to hurry towards the house, but before they reached it a short, stocky, fair-haired man came running out and into both their minds sprang the name McFee. He ran towards them, his expression one of absolute fright. Close upon him, though moving with less freedom, came an old man, repeatedly looking behind him.

Two or three other people followed, whom neither Cousins nor Cunningham identified in any way, and bringing up the rear came the red-haired youth. By then Cunningham and Cousins were outside the gate.

The youth called loudly:

'Get the people out of that house, for heaven's sake!'

He pointed to the house on the right of the hotel, and ran towards one on the other side, shouting as he went:

'Fire—fire!'

Cunningham and Cousins regarded each other, startled. There was no wisp of smoke, no hint of flame, but the word echoed high about the street, causing people hurrying to and from the station to stop and stare towards them. After a moment of indecision, Cunningham moved towards the next-door house, saying sharply:

'He must know something.'

'Yes, but—'

Cunningham was out of earshot, and began to thunder on the knocker of the next-door house. Cousins, a little slower, was standing outside the Brittling Hotel when he heard the roar.

It was the last thing he heard: he just caught a glimpse of a terrific sheet of flame, and then felt a sharp pain at the back of his head. He fell, inert and unconscious, while the house went upwards, pieces of stone and masonry, glass, wood and steel, flying in all directions. Smoke and dust rose up and covered that section of the road like a pall. A few men and women came staggering out of it, the foremost being the red-haired youth carrying a child.

Cousins did not appear, but Cunningham came, half supporting an old woman. He saw the rubble immediately outside what had been the front door of the hotel, knowing that Neil had been there and must be buried beneath it. From somewhere amid the ruins came a bluish flame, which flickered and went out, but was revived again farther away.

Uniformed men told him to move back to safety, but he took no notice, tearing at the rubble, untouched by the possibility of an explosion, which increased with every passing minute. Tight-lipped, hard-eyed, Cunningham toiled on, the people who had run in such frenzied haste from the Brittling Hotel completely forgotten.

CHAPTER FOUR

NO ROOM FOR DOUBT

Cunningham walked stiffly up the stairs to Dawlish's flat. He had not washed, his clothes were torn and dirty, his face black, his finger-nails broken and the skin of his hands torn in a dozen places. Felicity opened the door, Dawlish behind her. Her lips parted, but no words came. With a sudden movement Dawlish lunged past her and took Cunningham's arm. He led him into the flat, lowered him into a chair.

Cunningham's words, flat and expressionless, broke the silence. 'Neil's dead.'

Dawlish said nothing, but turned for whisky and glasses. He mixed a stiff drink which his friend took without a word, and swallowed at a gulp.

Words seemed to mean nothing. The thing which mattered to Dawlish was that while he had been out on a trifling errand, Neil Cousins had been killed. He knew nothing of it beyond Cunningham's brief statement, but already he blamed himself. He should not have sent them, they were not used to the kind of emergency he knew so well. They had gone into the affair with high spirits, but no training. Babes to the slaughter.

Training and experience might have saved Neil. *He* might have saved Neil. It was a forbidding thought, one which Dawlish could not get out of his mind.

Neither he nor Felicity tried to prompt Cunningham, who remained silent for some minutes. Then:

'We went along and saw the place. Nothing special. Red-head went in there, and one of us was going to 'phone. Then the people started to stream out, all of Felicity's visitors and some others. Red-head came out bellowing "fire", and told us to get the people out of the house next door. I went to try, Neil was slow off the mark. The place was blown up, and he was under the wreckage. They got him out half an hour ago.'

'No hope at all?'

'The doctors say he was killed instantaneously,' said Cunningham in a harsh voice. 'I hope he was, he—' he gulped, and then stood up abruptly. 'I'd better have a bath.' Blindly, he went towards the bathroom.

Felicity and Dawlish exchanged glances, and then Dawlish followed his friend, ran a warm bath, put out towels and made sure that Cunningham had everything he wanted. Cunningham said nothing. The others knew that he and Cousins had been close friends for many years, that there had been a bond between them that they had believed nothing would break. They could imagine how Cunningham was feeling then, although they knew that in time he would recover, and also that he would want to go into this affair with both feet to avenge his friend's death.

Felicity said quietly:

'There's no room for doubt about it now.'

'No-o,' said Dawlish with an effort. 'I was slow, too slow. My God, I shouldn't have sent them.'

'Even if it's true,' said Felicity crisply, 'there's nothing you can do about it.'

Dawlish looked at her with a bleak smile. 'That's common-sense, of course. You're right.' He helped himself to a whisky and soda. 'No room for doubt, and we're right in it. I'll have to tell Trivett of the tie-up, of course, but—'

'Is there any "but" about that, now?'

'Well, yes,' said Dawlish. 'This fits in with everything else. A bunch of people think that I can help them. We've proof enough now that they had reason for needing help, but we don't know that they'll confide in the police. They might in me. The question is, how to get in touch with them?'

'I wonder if you're right, Pat,' said Felicity slowly. 'Supposing the man who wants you interested arranged the blowing up, and—and hoped you'd be there.'

'It could be, but it's not my bet,' said Dawlish. 'Somebody was after the Brittling Hotel crowd. Red-head discovered this, and got them out in time. He's shown up well. The thing is, what's to do if Trivett comes?' He hesitated, then went on: 'I think I'll nip out the back way if he comes. Just for a start I'd like to hear what these people have to say before contacting him.'

He started, at a ring from the telephone, and stepped towards it.

He half-expected to hear Trivett's voice asking him whether he knew what had happened at the Brittling Hotel, but it was not Trivett. The voice which spoke in an oddly matter-of-fact tone was that of the red-headed boy.

'Listen, Captain Dawlish, you know what happened at Bayswater, don't you?'

Dawlish said sharply: 'Yes.'

'I couldn't help it,' the youth assured him earnestly. 'I did everything I could to stop it, I even warned your friends. You must know that.'

'I know,' said Dawlish.

'Well, look here, I want to see you. It's urgent. Nothing will happen to you, you needn't take any notice of what I said to your girl friend, I was only trying to get you interested. Don't think I'm trying to double-cross you.' The youth hesitated and then went on: 'You know Yvonne Lejeune? Well, I sent her, too. I can't tell the police about this, but you *might* be able to help.' There was a note of appeal as the voice went on: 'We've tried every way we can to get you to help, but we can't do anything more.'

Dawlish said stiffly:

'Where can I see you?'

'Do you know Woking at all?'

'A little.'

'There's a house just outside the town, on the Common, near the golf-course. Course Cottage, any cabby will tell you. Can you come out tonight? I do assure you that I'm not trying to trick you.'

'Thanks,' said Dawlish dryly. 'I'll be there.'

The voice sharpened. 'You'll play straight? No police?'

'No police,' said Dawlish.

He put the receiver down and turned to find Felicity looking at him fixedly.

'I don't know whether he's just young or very ingenuous,' he said. 'You gathered that he gave me an address and made me swear not to take the police along?' She nodded, and he went on: 'If he's right, they've tried all manner of tricks to get me to see them, and now they feel that the situation's desperate.'

'It looks it,' said Felicity.

'H'm. If they've a story that is worth it all, it'll be good hearing,' said Dawlish. 'Is Joan coming in tonight?'

'She should be here any time,' said Felicity.

'You won't be alone then. Good,' said Dawlish crisply. 'Andy will want to come, I'd better go and see whether he's all right.'

He had withdrawn within himself, Felicity saw, and she imagined that he was thinking far less of the death of Neil Cousins than of what the red-headed youth had said.

Dawlish went in search of Cunningham, and found him towelling vigorously.

'Red-head says he's at a house near Woking, and I've promised to go to see him tonight. If you'd rather stay here—'

'Don't be an idiot!' exclaimed Cunningham, 'I'm coming.' They both looked at the heap of tattered clothes that lay on a chair.

'Some of mine will do for tonight,' said Dawlish. 'We'll have a snack before we go, and then catch a fast train to Woking.' He brought a dressing-gown from his bedroom and tossed it into the bathroom, and then laid a suit out. He was relieved to find Cunningham reacting so well. The first hurdle was over, and the rest would be easier.

Before they had finished a meal of bread and cheese and coffee, Joan Tennant, the friend who shared the flat with them, had come in. If she noticed any strain in the atmosphere she made no comment, and went to her own room before the two men were ready. They put on overcoats, Dawlish handing his Service revolver to Cunningham, and slipping a small automatic into his own pocket.

'I feel better with that,' admitted Cunningham.

'I don't think we'll need 'em,' said Dawlish briefly, 'but we can't afford to be caught napping.' He turned to Felicity and went on: 'We should be back by midnight, but if we aren't, we'll give you a ring. Bye, darling.' He glanced at Joan's door and fancied that he heard a snort from behind it, and then with Cunningham went out of the flat by the back way.

There was no moon, and it was very dark. A brooding silence hung over the city, occasionally broken by the rasping note of a bus changing gear. They walked briskly towards a taxi rank where one cab was waiting.

The cabby, a dark, vague figure, opened the door of the vehicle. Dawlish shone his flashlight into the interior of the cab, before stepping in.

'Why that caution?' asked Cunningham as they settled down.

'Someone could have been waiting for us,' said Dawlish.

He looked out of the rear window, but no lights followed the cab. He was on edge, expecting developments at any moment, and yet trying to convince himself that so far the only people who knew that he was becoming involved were the motley collection represented by the red-head.

What manner of people were they to have a youth of seventeen or eighteen as their spokesman?

The cabby drew up at Waterloo, and together Dawlish and Cunningham groped their way towards the booking-hall. They were lucky, for a fast train to Woking was due to start in ten minutes. It was already in, and despite the darkness of the night, crowded, but they found seats opposite each other.

They could not exchange confidences, and Dawlish reflected on the fact that had he been on official business he could have travelled by car, and saved both time and anxiety. It might be possible, after the interview, to bring the affair within the orbit of his particular branch of the Intelligence Department, or at least the police. Yet the insistence of the red-head and others on avoiding the police made him wonder whether it would be wise.

He would, however, pay little attention to prejudices. If he decided to become involved, these people would have to leave him to assess the situation and make what decisions he felt were justified.

The train moved off. The first stop seemed a long while

coming, but at last they climbed out at Woking, groping their way towards the station yard, where they were lucky enough to get a taxi. 'Course Cottage, near the golf-course,' directed Dawlish. 'Do you know it?'

'Oh, yessir.' There was no hesitation in the cabby's manner, and Dawlish wondered why the cottage should be so well known. He made another quick survey of the inside of the cab before getting in; all the time he was conscious of a feeling that he was being observed.

Cunningham said unexpectedly:

'Eyes seem to be looking at us from everywhere.'

'Ye-es. I didn't fancy you felt like that too,' said Dawlish. 'It's imagination, I fancy.'

The journey to the cottage was not a long one. There was no light at the house and except for the lights of the cab, now fast disappearing, nothing to relieve the darkness of the porch.

Dawlish shone his flashlight, and located the bell-push. He pressed, but there was no immediate answer. He pressed again, and Cunningham muttered an imprecation. Then:

'They can't have been fooling us?'

'There's no point in it,' said Dawlish. 'But they might have had another scare here, and cleared out.'

'Nice thought,' commented Cunningham glumly. 'Keep your finger on the damned thing!'

Instead Dawlish located a knocker, and thundered on the door. This time there was a response, for shuffling footsteps came to their ears, and soon they heard the clanking of a chain being removed from the door.

CHAPTER FIVE

COURSE COTTAGE

As he heard the chain being withdrawn, and the door opening, Dawlish switched on his torch and shone it on the face of a man who had every aspect of an octogenarian. It glistened on his bald head and eyes which blinked in the sudden light.

'Please, sir, please!' he said.

Dawlish, after seeing the ancient, expected a quivering falsetto, but Felicity had warned him and he should have been prepared. This man, presumably Mr Richard Playfair, had a deep, mellow voice which echoed about the small porch and the hall beyond.

Dawlish switched off the torch.

'Thank you,' said Mr Playfair, 'I am always affected by bright lights. May I ask your name?'

'Dawlish,' said Dawlish.

'Indeed,' exclaimed Playfair, 'indeed, sir, I am delighted! So you have come. Until the last moment I was afraid that your good sense, as you would doubtless term it, would dissuade you. Really, I am delighted. Please come in.'

He stepped aside. Dawlish put his right hand to his pocket

about the automatic, for there was something eerie about this reception. The faint light coming from a small lamp burning under a heavy blue shade, was only enough to show the old man's figure in vague outline.

The door closed, and, by sense of touch, Playfair replaced the chain.

'We feel so much more secure after taking that precaution, gentlemen,' said Playfair. 'After our experience earlier in the day, I am sure that you will understand that. May I ask—' he hesitated, and then added a little diffidently: 'May I ask whom you have brought with you, Captain Dawlish? I believe that our young friend *did* stipulate that there should be no association with the police at this juncture.'

Dawlish said: 'There are no police here.'

'Thank you, Captain Dawlish. How refreshing it is to meet a man of his word—both refreshing and rare. Please follow me.' The old fellow picked up the lamp, and walked along the wide hall of the cottage to a door beneath the stairs. He coughed, a little apologetically.

'We try to make *quite* sure that we are not assaulted, you see, and the Company has decided to have its rehearsals in the cellar for a little while to come. Believe me,' added Playfair earnestly, 'the cellar has been adapted, and is most comfortable. If you will wait just a moment, I will switch on the light.'

Dawlish and Cunningham made no comment, until the old man had gone unsteadily half-way down stairs which faded into darkness beyond the radius of the blue light. Then:

'Rehearsals!' whispered Cunningham. 'Is he sane?'

'We ought to find out soon,' said Dawlish.

He kept his right hand on his gun, and then blinked in the sudden light. It came from an unshaded electric bulb at the foot of the stairs.

Playfair peered up at them.

'Please don't feel in any way apprehensive, I am aware that this procedure is a little unusual, but we have had such a trying time. And we are anxious not to waste more, you understand, it is so important that we get ready for the first performance. Are you interested in theatricals, Captain Dawlish?'

'Not yet,' admitted Dawlish.

'Not yet?' Playfair peered up at them. 'Of course, of course, you expect to be interested in us! Well, I hope you will be, Captain Dawlish, goodness knows that we have done everything possible to ensure your interest.'

At the foot of the stairs were two doors. Playfair turned the handle of the larger of the two, and immediately a voice could be heard declaiming:

'*It is impossible. No one with ordinary decency would try to force it!*'

'*Indeed, sir,*' came another voice, thinner and carrying with it a note of menace. '*I hope that you will think better of your decision.*'

There was a pause, and then Playfair said mildly:

'I think we should stop now, ladies and gentleman, our visitor has arrived. We can proceed afterwards, of course; you need not consider the evening wasted. Captain Dawlish, I have not the privilege of knowing your friend. If I may have his name I will perform the introductions.'

Dawlish said faintly: 'Major Andrew Cunningham.'

'Thank you. Ladies and gentlemen, allow me to present Major Cunningham and Captain Dawlish.'

Playfair raised his arm in a grandiloquent gesture, and Dawlish and Cunningham stepped through.

The room was unexpectedly large, and looked bare in spite of some dozen occupants. Two of them were standing in the middle of the room, each holding a folio of typescript. Most of the others, also with folios, were sitting about the walls. Amongst them Dawlish recognized Yvonne Lejeune, *petite* and attractive. She was sitting beside the red-haired youth. An astonishingly fat man sat at a piano, his hands poised above the keys.

'There you are!' exclaimed the red-haired youth triumphantly. 'I said we'd get him! Captain Dawlish, I always believed you would help us!'

Dawlish eyed him grimly.

'And so I might, if I know what all this flummery is about,' he said.

'Well, we can't stop working just because of the trouble, can we? Would *you* stop the war just because things weren't going right?' He delivered himself of that question with conscious righteousness, and then continued: 'I would have seen you in the other room, but I wanted all the others to know you, so that there couldn't be any chance of a mistake in future. I don't think they'll mistake you for anyone else, now! Eh, folks?'

The 'folks' were staring pointedly at Dawlish and Cunningham. There were four women, three of them little more than girls, and five men, as well as Playfair and the youth. One of the men was short, stocky, and fair-haired.

'McFee,' thought Dawlish. 'What crazy business is this?'

He noticed a tall, angular woman in a tweed coat, and recognized Miss Phoebe Lancaster; Felicity's descriptions had all been remarkably accurate. He was, to put it mildly, taken aback. He had expected to find them all frightened and excited, talking only of the nearness of their escape: yet here they were rehearsing a play, and not much of a play at that, if the lines he had heard were any indication of its merit.

The red-haired youth said:

'Now you've seen everyone, perhaps you'll come with me, Mr

Dawlish. I'm the manager, Dick Bowing,' he added ingenuously. 'I can speak for all of them, I know. Well, we'd better let them carry on.'

In a confused frame of mine Dawlish followed Dick Bowing through a further door, which Cunningham closed behind them. They stepped into a smaller room, furnished comfortably, but a little oddly. Bowing waved them hospitably to chairs.

'Make yourselves comfy, gentlemen. I always think it's better to be comfortable when you talk, don't you?' He took a large-bowled pipe from his pocket and began to fill it.

Dawlish said sharply: 'I don't know whether you think I'm prepared to join you in a game, Bowing, but if you do, it's time you changed your mind. I've no time to waste. You ought to know why I'm here. One of my friends went to see you for me, this afternoon.'

'Two, I saw 'em,' said Bowing brightly.

'One was killed,' said Dawlish abruptly.

The smiling expression on the youngster's face faded. He looked suddenly an older man, prematurely aged. He licked his lips, regarding both Dawlish and Cunningham gravely. The room was very quiet; no sound came from next door.

'Yes, I know,' Bowing said. 'That's what I was talking about on the telephone. But it wasn't our fault, Captain Dawlish, and I did all I could. I was lucky to get away myself. And it's easy for you to get the impression that we're not really worried. The play was Playfair's idea. His aim was to give everyone something to take their mind off the main fact, Captain Dawlish. Every one of us—' he paused and then repeated emphatically: '*Every one* of us is frightened for his life. You may think that sounds dramatic, but there it is. None of us is safe, you know what happened at the hotel—that's the kind of thing that might happen to us anywhere.'

'Go on,' said Dawlish quietly.

'Believe me,' Bowing continued, 'it's no joke going *every-where* under the shadow of death. Yvonne told you, but when you made her go to the police she didn't say anything more. We *can't* say anything to the police yet, that's why we decided to try to get you interested.'

'Why me?' asked Dawlish.

'Well, hang it, you're just the kind of fellow we need,' Bowing said. 'I've read about you and your extraordinary adventures, you see. I know you're not above dodging the police, too, I knew a man on the *Echo*, and he gave me the inside story of one of your shows. When I remembered that, I said to the others: "If we can get this man Dawlish interested, we'll be all right."'

'Did you,' said Dawlish. 'Then isn't it time you were more explicit?'

'I'm going to be,' protested Bowing. 'The only thing is—*if* I tell you everything, will you promise to help us? I mean, I just daren't let you know unless you join us, and swear yourself to secrecy. And Major Cunningham also,' added Bowing, 'I can't tell you a thing unless I have your word. Just give it, and off I'll go on the story.'

CHAPTER SIX

BOWING TELLS THE TALE

Dawlish leaned back in his chair and eyed the young man, so eagerly waiting for a hearty signal of assent.

Cunningham stirred impatiently.

'Well, is that all right?' asked Bowing.

Dawlish spoke with deceptive mildness.

'I don't think you quite realize the position. If conditions are to be stipulated, then it is I who will stipulate them. I haven't come here to ask you to tell me your story, I've come here to get it whether you want to disclose it or not, and Major Cunningham and I will be the only judges of whether it should be passed on to the police or not.'

'Oh, no,' said Bowing, shaking his head. 'That won't do at all.'

'Before we come to blows,' said Dawlish mildly, 'let me inform you of one or two things. I am not a policeman, but I am an officer in His Majesty's Army, and any information lodged with me should be transmitted to my senior officers, if not to the police. If the circumstances made me decide to say nothing, it would be at considerable personal risk.'

'Now don't tell me that *that* would worry you,' said Bowing. 'Hang it, I've read about you! And I told you about—'

'Your friend on the *Echo*, yes,' said Dawlish. 'He only told you half the truth. There's another matter, which makes my interest keenly personal—the murder of Captain Cousins. I propose to find out who murdered him, and whether I have your help or not doesn't mean much either way. But,' continued Dawlish in a harder voice, 'if there is, the slightest hint of trouble from you, or of obstructiveness, you and your whole bunch will go to jail until the affair is over. There isn't time for playing hide-and-seek.'

'You said you hadn't brought a policeman with you!' flashed Bowing. 'Does that mean you're a liar?'

'It means that if you don't stop this nonsense I'll put you over my knee and tan your hide,' snapped Dawlish.

'Now steady, steady,' remonstrated Bowing, after a startled pause, 'I haven't said anything much, have I? I didn't think you'd act this way, but I suppose it's understandable enough. If—if I convince you that I'm wise not to tell the police yet, will you promise to say nothing? That's fair, surely?'

'Supposing you don't convince me?'

'That's up to me, isn't it?' demanded Bowing. 'If I can't make you see how necessary it is to say nothing, I shan't think much of myself. Now look here, we're all men of the world,' continued the youth with enormous assurance. 'We're prepared to take chances if the gamble's worth it—stake, I mean. I'll undertake to convince you, all right, and I'll show you the evidence. If you think the police ought to know after that, I'll give up. I will, honestly.'

To Dawlish, the amazing thing was the other's confidence. The irritation he had felt towards Bowing dissipated, and he found himself eagerly anticipating what the youngster had to say. It was unlikely that after so portentous a beginning, and so long and patient an attempt to enlist his help, that it would be an anti-climax.

He looked at Cunningham reflectively.

'What do you make of it, Andy?'

'We won't lose anything,' Cunningham said briefly.

'No-o. All right, Bowing, go ahead. If you convince us that you're right in keeping it from the police, I'll say nothing yet. But it will depend on the motive for your reticence. Personal reasons won't be good enough.'

'I should think not!' said Bowing warmly. 'Just a moment, while I light my pipe.'

He put a match to the enormous bowl, puffed great clouds of smoke into the air and then nodded with satisfaction.

'That's all right. Now answer me this, Captain Dawlish. To whom is the Police Force responsible for its actions?'

Dawlish said impatiently: 'The Home Office, of course.'

'Right. Now if I tell the police about this, the Home Office will have to know. I mean, I can't stipulate that the police don't pass anything on, can I? I see you agree with me there, anyhow. Well, I know that an important man at the Home Office is a Nazi spy, *and* two or three of the others.'

Bowing delivered himself of this statement with complete simplicity, nor did he appear to expect any reaction. Cunningham uttered a sharp exclamation, but Dawlish contrived to repress one, merely saying with some irony:

'Indeed?'

'Now you don't have to be so damned superior about it,' snapped Bowing. 'I admit I'm only a youngster, but I'm an Englishman, and the only thing I'm worried about just now is winning the war. The same goes for you, doesn't it?'

'It certainly does,' said Dawlish crisply. 'And if you've any evidence that people at the Home Office are Nazis, or Nazi agents, you've a case for saying nothing to the police.'

Bowing's resentment faded in a new eagerness.

'Now I knew I could rely on you! Listen, Captain Dawlish. All of those people next door work, or have worked, at the Home Office. Staying late, as we've sometimes done, we've seen and heard some pretty queer things. Maybe you didn't know about the list of suspected persons under the 18B Regulation, which was stolen. It was only lost for three days, but half-a-dozen ruddy Fascists had made a getaway by then, and the Home Office couldn't do a thing about it.'

Dawlish sat up abruptly.

Until that moment he had regarded Bowing with considerable suspicion and even more scepticism, but the statement shook him.

'Well, that was the point when we began to think,' continued the youth. 'You see, McFee and I worked in that Department. Moreover, we'd stayed overtime the night the list was stolen, and we'd been seen, so we came in for a lot of questioning. McFee went as far as to say they ought to look amongst the nobs for the spy, and they sacked him. But he was right. The man who stole that paper was Sir Alfred Clay.'

Having heard only vaguely of Sir Alfred Clay, Dawlish was not as impressed as Bowing obviously expected him to be.

'Why, don't you know him?' exclaimed Bowing. 'His office is next to ours, and one day Phoebe Lancaster saw him with a cake of soap in his hand standing at *our* door. She mentioned this to May Larkin who passed it on to me. Well, I've read a lot of crime stuff, and I wondered if Clay was up to mischief. So I managed to slip into his cloak-room the next day and I snaffled his soap.' Bowing pulled open a drawer and took out a large envelope. He opened it, extracted a cake of toilet soap and handed it to Dawlish. 'See that, Captain Dawlish. *The impression of a key!* It's been used since, and nearly washed out, but you can still see it all right.'

Dawlish could; and Cunningham leaned forward, his interest quickening.

'That's what they call Exhibit 1,' said Bowing with relish. 'But I nearly paid plenty for it, someone tried to push me under a bus that evening, and someone else was waiting for me in the room I had then, in Bloomsbury. Half-strangled me and then left me in the room with the gas turned on. I'm not joking, here's Exhibit 2.'

From the drawer he pulled out a smaller envelope, extracted a newspaper cutting and held it towards the others.

Dawlish read slowly:

YOUTH'S ALLEGATIONS STORY OF MYSTERIOUS
ASSAILANT

At Bow Street yesterday an eighteen-year-old youth, Richard Arthur Bowing, described as a clerk at the Home Office, was remanded for further inquiries after being charged with wilfully misleading the police. Bowing was found by a friend, Miss May Larkin, suffering from slight coal-gas poisoning in his room at Ley Court, Bloomsbury, and on the same evening lodged a complaint with the police to the effect that he had been attacked, half-strangled and left in his room with an unlighted gas stove turned on. In evidence, Det.-Sergeant Lockey, of the Bloomsbury Division, said that there was no evidence of a struggle and that the only finger-prints on the gas taps were identical with Bowing's. He had no hesitation in giving his opinion that Bowing himself had turned on the taps.

Dawlish and Cunningham read it, and then another cutting, pinned behind the first, stating that Bowing was fined £5 and warned that similar offences would be dealt with more severely.

As the two men looked up at the youngster, he said sharply:

'I don't know whether my finger-prints were on that tap or

not, but I do know I wasn't the last to turn it on. I was attacked all right, and if May hadn't turned up I'd have been a goner. What do you make of *that*, Captain Dawlish?'

'It certainly sounds interesting,' admitted Dawlish.

'I should say it was!' exclaimed Bowing. 'Well, after that I was asked to resign. I wouldn't, so I was sacked. McFee was gone by then, and May was transferred to another Department. I was pretty scared, I can tell you. Then old Playfair stepped in. He had always believed that there was something wrong at H.O. Some of us had lunched together in the same Lyons, and we got talking—you know how it is. Playfair, who has an interest in the Brittling Hotel, suggested that I should live there. McFee went along there too. Then May came along, and Phoebe. She used to be on the halls, you know, but she's getting past it, and we had a meeting at the Brittling to discuss things. We were all sure that Clay was our man, but junior clerks and typists can't do much against a fellow in *his* position.'

Bowing paused, and then went on:

'Why, none of us could even get an interview with the Chief about it! Playfair tried once or twice, but was always sidetracked. Then he was fired. He was supposed to have pinched some petty cash. The damned rogues!' added Bowing angrily, 'Playfair's as straight as they make 'em. It didn't matter what they did or said, you see, all they wanted to do was to blacken our characters and get us out of the H.O.'

'Are all of the people in the next room included?' asked Dawlish.

'All except Yvonne,' Bowing smiled widely. 'Pretty, isn't she? Well, the day Yvonne came along there was another shindy. Something else was stolen out of our Chief's office, and she was around. It turned up again on the floor in Clay's room, as a matter of fact, and of course he swore that he didn't know anything about it. Actually the old swab had taken it himself, and when it was missed so early, dropped it on the floor. Two or three of the people in his office are working with him, I don't think there's any doubt of that.'

'I still don't see how Yvonne joined up with you,' said Dawlish patiently.

'Well, Phoebe saw that she was in a pretty bad way, no friends or anything, and took her along to the Brittling,' said Bowing. 'Then we got talking—you know how it is after there's been a breeze of some kind. And Yvonne's had a nasty time in France. Lost her people in the early days, and two of her brothers are prisoners-of-war in Germany. She hates the very word "Nazi", and when she thought there was a chance of having a stab at some of them over here she was all for it. I sent her along to you,' added Bowing, 'I'd read and heard so much about you, and I thought if we could only get you to help we'd have a chance of doing something really useful.'

'How many of you had left the Home Office by then?' demanded Dawlish.

'Oh, all of us. And that was the queer thing about it, because usually it's ten times as hard to get out of the Service as it is to get in, especially in wartime. I don't mind telling you we were pretty scared. Clay knew we suspected him, you see, and he was after us—or some of his people were. Phoebe went for a few days' holiday down in Devon. Blow me if she wasn't pushed off a cliff—here's Exhibit 3.'

It was another newspaper cutting, and described a rescue off the Devon coast, in which Phoebe Lancaster had played the most prominent part.

'She didn't fall,' said Bowing earnestly, 'but she wasn't going to say that she was pushed, after what had happened to me. Then Mac got a job in a munitions factory, and nearly got blown up.

After that he was fired for being careless. So you see how serious it is. All of us have been attacked or threatened, sometimes by telephone, sometimes with anonymous letters. I've got a bunch of them here, but I won't worry you with them yet. You can see how it's taking shape, can't you?'

Dawlish nodded.

'I was pretty sure you would,' said Bowing with evident satisfaction. He flushed a little. 'As a matter of fact I rather stood or fell by you, Captain Dawlish. McFee and one or two of the others wanted to go to a Detective Agency, but I wasn't having any. Things were getting far too desperate for that. Wherever we went we were followed, and it got on our nerves. Anyway, we had to do *some*thing. Besides, I guessed that sooner or later they'd have a real go at us.'

Bowing paused, and then drew a deep breath.

'And that's exactly what they did—but you know about that. I know it all sounds a pretty tall story, but there it is. The only people we could turn to were the police, and where would that get us? I've already given evidence about the soap, and not been believed. And Clay would be warned, while most of us would probably be put into jail for making false charges. This had to be handled differently, and I went all out to get you interested.'

Dawlish said quietly: 'Are you *quite* sure it's Clay?'

'It's Clay all right,' said Bowing. 'I've seen him at the Chief's safe. Well, let's get on.' Bowing took his pipe from lips, as if relieved that it had gone out. 'I've gone around watching one or two of these fellows. There was one man who was always outside the Brittling, a big chap with enormous shoulders I named the Ox. I don't know whether he knows I've been following *him* sometimes, but today I went up to his flat. It's in Cromwell Road.'

'I had a bit of luck,' Bowing admitted brightly. 'The people in the next flat had gone out, and their door wasn't locked. I heard the Ox and several others talking, and they seemed pretty pleased with themselves. They said something about the place going up today. I didn't know what they meant until I caught a glimpse of two of them. *They'd been working in the cellar at the Brittling all that day.* Strewth! I just jumped out of that flat and rushed along to the hotel quicker than you can say "Knife". Then I started yelling fire, and got most of the people out of the houses next door.'

Dawlish sat silent for a moment deep in thought. Then he said abruptly: 'Give me the address of the Ox, and the names of all your people here, and I'll get in touch with you again tomorrow.'

Bowing pulled a list from the open drawer. 'Here are the names, and the Ox lives at 912A, Cromwell Road. The tenant of the flat is a Mrs Cromarty.' Bowing smoothed his hair back, and then stood up. 'You don't know how much good you've done me, Captain Dawlish! I felt kind of responsible for having these people on my hands, and—well, you know what it's like. If old Playfair hadn't thought of doing the play, and giving us something to think about, we would all have been haywire by now. He wrote it, by the way, and although I don't think much of it we've had some good times at rehearsal.'

'Playfair said something about the first performance,' said Dawlish.

'He's an optimist!' chuckled Bowing. 'As a matter of fact we're going to get a hall and put the show on as soon as we've got everything cleared up. Playfair thinks it won't be long—but he's a believer in miracles.'

'He needs to be,' said Dawlish dryly, 'I haven't heard anything quite like it before.'

He stopped abruptly.

Across his words came a loud, high-pitched whistling sound,

uncannily like the sound of a bomb's descent. It made all of them jump, and Bowing's expression changed to one of sharp concern.

'That's the alarm,' he snapped. 'They've found us!'

The door leading to the other room opened, and McFee and Yvonne stood on the threshold, startled and afraid.

'Can you hear that?'

It was an unnecessary question, for the noise was echoing loudly about the rooms, almost drowning the words. They hurried towards the door leading to the stairs. There was a picture beside it, and this Bowing took down revealing a bell-push. He pressed it, and a section of the wall opened.

'Through here,' he urged hurriedly. 'We can get out through the garden.'

The play readers went through quickly enough, and then Bowing turned to Dawlish. 'Time we were off too, Cap'pen!'

'We're staying,' said Dawlish briefly.

'Staying?' echoed Bowing. 'But—' he paused, and then a grin of what appeared to be sheer delight crossed his features. 'My hat, you're going to have a stab at them! I'm in this!' He pressed the bell-push again, and the sliding door closed.

Footsteps could be heard immediately above them.

'Well, shall we go up to them, or wait here?' asked Bowing in a hushed voice.

Dawlish said nothing, but quietly taking an automatic from his pocket moved to the bottom stair.

CHAPTER SEVEN

FIRST ENCOUNTER

Dawlish moved up the stairs swiftly, making little sound. Cunningham followed, and Bowing brought up the rear. The footsteps continued to echo above them, and Dawlish felt puzzled because the intruders took so little trouble to hide their presence.

He reached the door.

He was half-prepared for it to open before he touched the handle, but it did not. The automatic in his right hand, he opened the door an inch, and then stood quite still. He caught a glimpse of a man walking away from him. The powerful shoulders were exceptionally broad, and to his mind there sprang the soubriquet 'the Ox'. There was a gun in his hand. The man spoke in a hoarse whisper which travelled vaguely to Dawlish's ears.

'See anything?'

'Not yet.' Whoever answered was out of sight. The Ox moved away. Dawlish widened the door opening and slipped into the hall.

He glanced swiftly along the passage in either direction, seeing that the front door was closed, and that no one was in sight. Creaking above his head told him that the intruders were going up the stairs.

Going slowly forward, he was in time to see two men disappear along a passage on the first floor. Dawlish beckoned to his companions, who joined him with commendable silence.

'Look in the nearer rooms,' he said quietly.

There were four other doors, and Bowing went to the two nearest, Cunningham to those farthest away, while Dawlish watched the top of the stairs.

Bowing returned first.

'Both empty. What's next?'

'Keeping still,' said Dawlish, and then Cunningham rejoined them, shaking his head to indicate that no one was in the other rooms. Dawlish went on: 'Where is the kitchen?'

'I've been there,' said Cunningham. 'The back door's locked on the inside.'

Peering along the hall, Dawlish frowned.

'The front door isn't, but we saw Playfair lock it. Or we heard him put the chain up,' he amended.

'Look here, what's next?' began Bowing. 'I mean—'

'Hush!' said Dawlish. 'Don't make a shindy, but keep close against the wall beneath the staircase. Andy, slip into that room and keep the door ajar, will you?' He indicated a room immediately near the foot of the stairs, and then joined Bowing. Both were crouched low.

They could hear the stealthy footsteps upstairs, but nothing else for a long time. Bowing stirred, impatiently. There was no sound from the room where Andy was waiting, and Dawlish wished heartily that Bowing was not with them, for he could see that his eagerness might prove disastrous.

Then, quite clearly, he heard a cry.

It was short and sharp, and broke off suddenly.

'Who's that?' gasped Bowing.

'For God's sake keep quiet,' hissed Dawlish.

Bowing glared at him angrily, but obeyed. There was silence from upstairs for a while, but it was soon broken by stealthy footsteps and whispering voices.

Dawlish waited with his gun poised.

The talkers came down the stairs, and a gruff voice said:

'She's heavier than she looks.'

'You 'aven't croaked 'er, 'ave you?' the other demanded.

'Serve 'er right if I 'ave. But she'll come round, the Boss will want to talk to 'er. I wonder where the other coves are?'

'There's a cellar, ain't there?'

Waiting, Dawlish saw, sideways on, the man with the big shoulders appear. Beneath his arms were a pair of slim, shapely legs. It was easy to see that the two men were carrying a girl between them.

As they rounded the last stair, they came face to face with the muzzle of Dawlish's gun.

'Gently, now,' said Dawlish softly. 'Don't drop her.'

The man with the big shoulders gasped, and released the girl's legs. The other man stood as if petrified. Between them the girl slid to the ground and they saw it was Yvonne.

'You might as well put your hands up,' said Dawlish casually to the big man. 'I don't want this gun to go off, but if it does, it will do so very efficiently. Stand against the wall, the two of you.'

They obeyed, moving like marionettes. Yvonne's body lay inertly on the carpet. Dawlish saw an ugly red mark on her forehead. Bowing muttered a high-pitched oath and moved towards her.

The two roughnecks stood with their backs against the wall, eyeing Dawlish's gun.

'All right, Andy,' said Dawlish composedly, and Cunningham

came out, his gun steady in his hand. 'We've caught a brace of them, but there might be others.'

He looked steadily at the two men, the one so aptly named Ox, the other, smaller and more nondescript with a scar on the left side of his face, then turned to Bowing and Cunningham. 'Andy, carry Yvonne downstairs, will you? Bowing, you lead the way. You'll follow,' he added harshly to the others. 'And if you know what's good for you, without a single squeal.' The strange little procession started immediately.

'The small room, I think,' directed Dawlish. It was suitable enough. The three men, after making Yvonne comfortable, arranged themselves in easy-chairs. The two prisoners were ranged against the wall.

Dawlish leaned over Yvonne, and felt her pulse: it was beating regularly. He did not think that there was much the matter with her, and put aside, for the moment, the question of how she had re-entered the house, as he turned to the Ox and his companion.

'What are your names?' he asked sharply.

Neither man spoke.

'Now get this fact clear,' said Dawlish, with assumed patience, 'we haven't a lot of time, and I don't propose to waste it. You'll answer my questions without delay, or you'll be marched off to the police. What are your names?'

'Dibben,' said the Ox, sullenly.

'Cromarty,' said the other.

'Cromarty! The same as the woman at the flat!' exclaimed Bowing.

The smaller of the prisoners glared at him with such malignance that the youngster seemed to be struck by a physical blow. His excitement vanished, and he drew back scared and ill-at-ease. Dawlish went on:

'Empty your pockets, both of you.'

He knew, as well as Cunningham, that he was giving them an opportunity for pulling guns, if they carried them; and watched them narrow-eyed. They took out wallets and various oddments, but each kept his hand away from his right-hand coat pocket. Dawlish waited until Dibben had finished, then calmly leaned forward and extracted a gun. Cromarty made a swift effort to keep his own gun hidden, but Dawlish knocked his hand away and extracted that also.

'You really mustn't play tricks,' he said gently. 'Andy, have a look through their wallets for anything of interest.' He kept his eyes fixed on Dibben, believing that the ox-like man would be the first of the two to crack. 'Dibben, who employs you?'

'We're not squealing!' Cromarty growled.

'No?' said Dawlish. 'I'm sure you'll reconsider that decision.'

'Don't say a word to 'im!' snarled Cromarty, swinging round on Dibben. 'If you do you'll get—'

Dawlish stood up again, approaching the men slowly. He did nothing, but the fear that he might, wiped the colour from Cromarty's face.

Dawlish stood back and regarded Dibben steadily.

'Who employs you?' he asked gently.

Dibben muttered: 'I—I dunno 'is name.'

'Who pays you?'

Again the big man licked his lips, and then said in a swift, whining voice:

'A man named Ketch, I dunno who he works for, he pays me, that's all I know. I can't tell you nuffink more, I can't tell you a fing!' His eyes were glittering and he looked thoroughly frightened. 'I just do what I'm told, thassal. I was told to come 'ere and see who was around, an'—'

He paused, for Dawlish to interpolate:

'Take them, or some of them, to the Boss. I heard you say so. Where were you going to take her?'

'To—to 'is flat.' Dibben pointed to Cromarty.

'And who was going to meet you there? The generous Mr Ketch?'

'Yes. Listen, I don't know 'oo you are, but I'm telling you all I can, see. I can't do no more than that, you can't expect me to!'

'You mustn't be surprised if I expect a lot of things,' said Dawlish. 'Certainly I don't think you've been completely frank with me, Dibben. How did you know that anyone was here?'

'K-Ketch told me.'

'When?'

'A coupla hours ago, I s'pose. I'm telling you all I can,' the Ox repeated, and he looked frightened out of his life. 'I can't do no more than that, I never wanted to come, I never—'

'Wanted to put high-explosive beneath the Brittling Hotel,' said Dawlish coldly. 'But you did.'

'I didn't! That was Cromarty an'—'

Dawlish, watching Cromarty out of the corner of his eyes, saw the man draw his leg back, but was too late to prevent him kicking Dibben in the ankle. The crack of leather on bone echoed loudly, and Dibben squealed with pain; then fell to one side, striking his head against the side of the bureau.

'I don't mind which of you comes across,' said Dawlish mildly, 'but I am going to have the answers, now, is Ketch your leader?'

'I—I reckon so,' Cromarty muttered. 'But you won't catch Ketch, yer ruddy nark. He's got it all covered.'

'A clever gentleman,' said Dawlish amiably, 'I must meet him. You were to report at Cromwell Road, taking any victims you could with you, I gather. Or was your choice to be selective?'

Cromarty muttered: 'Yeah. The red-head, and the skirt.'

'Well, well.' Dawlish turned to Cunningham. 'Anything in those wallets, Andy?'

'Not really.' Cunningham shook his head.

Dawlish looked at Yvonne, and saw that it would not be long before she came round. What to do with her? He did not think that she could be left at the cottage, even with Andy and Bowing: it might be the scene of more trouble before the night was out, and if that happened he was by no means sure that they would get away unscathed.

'Yvonne could go to my flat,' he mused. 'But the others—'

'What's the matter with the police?' suggested Cunningham, who seemed to guess what he was thinking.

'Here, that's out,' exclaimed Bowing. 'If you want somewhere to keep them, though, I know just the place.'

'You know the answer to everything, don't you,' said Dawlish dryly.

Bowing appeared to take the words at their face value, for he grinned with pleasure.

'You've said it, believe me!' He leaned forward with an air of conspiracy. 'Not far from here there's a little place where McFee has some friends, and he and the others are there now. As a matter of fact it's his house, and he let it when he started work at the H.O. There's a good-sized woodshed in the garden.'

'How long will it take us to get there?'

'About a quarter of an hour.'

It was better than nothing, but Dawlish was not too happy about it. There was a definite possibility that the grounds had been watched, and visitors followed to the house belonging to McFee. On the other hand there was not much time to spare. He said irresolutely: 'It'll mean the thin end of the stick for you, Andy. I'll want someone around the woodshed.'

'I can come with you, Captain Dawlish, can't I?' put in Bowing eagerly. 'I wouldn't miss it for the world.'

Dawlish eyed him judiciously, and then said:

'Only if you keep quiet. If you're going to shout advice and comments throughout any interviews, I'd rather you stayed behind.'

'I'll be as quiet as an oyster,' Bowing assured him warmly. 'What about Yvonne, will you take her with us to McFee's place?'

'No,' said Dawlish. 'To mine.'

The move proved easier and more straightforward than Dawlish had expected. McFee's little place was on the other side of the golf-course, the woodshed was a large one, and had a window which was blacked-out with brown paper. Inside it were a couple of clothes lines with which Dawlish and Cunningham made a workmanlike job of binding the prisoners; they uttered no protest, only a single outburst of obscenity from Cromarty, which stopped abruptly when Dawlish poked his automatic into the man's ribs.

Bowing and Andy went into the house, returning to report that all the others had reached there safely. Andy looked glum at the prospect of staying to keep his eyes on the house and the prisoners, but his 'cheer-ho' was hearty enough when Yvonne, Dawlish and Bowing left.

The return journey took longer than they expected and it was a quarter to twelve when they reached Waterloo.

At five past the hour Dawlish entered his flat, to find Felicity and Joan still up. Dawlish stayed only for a few minutes, explaining enough to make Felicity realize that a visit to Cromwell Road was inevitable. He touched lightly on the fact that Yvonne had been knocked out, and that she might derive more benefit from a good sleep than anything else.

'I don't have to say "be careful", do I?' Felicity said as she went with Dawlish and Bowing to the door. Dawlish kissed her in answer, inwardly cursing Bowing's limpet-like faithfulness and lack of tact. He led the youth in silence to the waiting taxi.

'Now we won't be long,' said Bowing joyously.

'Have you paused to think that this might be our last jaunt?' demanded Dawlish, with a touch of malice.

'By George, so it might!' exclaimed Bowing brightly. 'I would be as scared as blazes if I was on my own, but it's quite different with you.'

Dawlish swallowed hard, wondering whether the blarney was deliberate or spontaneous. He decided that in any case Bowing was irrepressible, and instructed the cabby to go to 950 Cromwell Road. To his credit, Bowing did not correct him, but when they had settled in the taxi said that he supposed Dawlish didn't want anyone to know that they were really going to 912A. Dawlish grunted agreement, and closed his eyes while the taxi sped on through the black-out.

CHAPTER EIGHT

JACK KETCH

'I know the place blind-folded,' said Bowing, 'you needn't worry. The front door's always on the latch, even by night. Cromarty lives on the first floor.' Dawlish grunted, wishing fervently that he was on his own.

He had told the cabby to wait farther along the road, and had paid the man well enough to ensure his patience. Along the dark thoroughfare and through the quiet of the night, he and Bowing walked quickly to Number 912A. Bowing, eagerly leading, pushed open the door. There was no need, at this juncture, for quietness, and Dawlish walked naturally up the stairs.

'How do they usually knock?' he demanded, 'a few hearty bangs, or a tap or two?'

'Wouldn't they have keys?' asked Bowing.

'They hadn't any with them,' Dawlish pointed out. He lifted the knocker and rapped three times. He heard a bolt being pushed back, and then a streamer of light came through the door. A woman's voice said:

'Is that you, Pete?'

Without waiting for an answer the woman widened the door.

Dawlish guessed that she was Cromarty's wife, but spent little time pondering that or anything else. He shot out a hand and gripped the woman's throat, stifling her startled cry. Deftly he pulled a handkerchief from his pocket and stuffed it expertly into her mouth.

He made little sound as he stretched the woman on the floor, and then took a length of cord from his pocket. Bowing's eyes started from his head at the speed with which Dawlish looped the cord about her wrists and ankles.

There were four doors leading from the hall, and beneath one of them was a sliver of light. Keeping his hand on the butt of his gun Dawlish opened it cautiously.

'Come on, come on,' a man said testily. 'Where the hell have you been?'

'Not very far away,' said Dawlish pleasantly. He took out his gun with a casual movement, assessing the two occupants of the room in a single glance.

They stared at him, transfixed.

They were sitting at a small table, whereon were two glasses, half-filled, a bottle of whisky and a syphon of soda. Their hands, holding cigarettes, stayed motionless.

'Well, well,' said Dawlish. 'This is no kind of welcome. Bowing, go and tap their pockets for guns, will you?'

The surprise was so complete that neither of the men spoke or moved until Bowing had taken automatics from their hip-pockets. Then the nearer man to Dawlish cleared his throat.

'Who—who—'

'I'm working *incognito*,' said Dawlish blandly, 'and I thought you'd prefer me to come without sending a wire.' He eyed them speculatively, wondering which was Ketch. Both were about fifty, both well-dressed.

Dawlish said abruptly: 'Which of you is Ketch?'

Neither of them spoke; the effect of surprise was even more remarkable than at the cottage. These two seemed no more self-possessed than Cromarty and Dibben. Yet there was a difference: the horror, even stupefaction, was fading from their eyes.

Dawlish shrugged his shoulders.

'You seem to be of the same breed as Dibben and Cromarty,' he commented. 'It took a little longer than it need have done, but both spoke in the end. Which of you is Ketch?'

The better-looking man said:

'I am. What's it to you?'

He leaned forward and picked up his glass, then tossed the contents down his throat. His hand was a little unsteady, but clearly his courage and self-possession were returning.

'Not much,' agreed Dawlish, 'but I would like to see your wallet. Take it out.'

The man stared at him, and for a moment it looked as if he would refuse, then slowly he obeyed, throwing the wallet on to the table.

Dawlish picked it up, leafing through it. There were cards and a letter. The cards were engraved: '*Jack Ketch*', and beneath them the words: '*Commission Agent*'. Dawlish smiled. 'Jack Ketch, a historic name. You wouldn't be the executioner for your friend Clay, would you?'

Ketch shrugged: 'I've never heard of any Clay.'

'I'll have to arrange an introduction,' said Dawlish gravely. 'From what I can gather you ought to get to know each other. You don't seem to be any luckier than your pals Dibben and Cromarty, for Mr Bowing and his friends, despite their attention, remain at large, and still thirsting for vengeance.'

Ketch eyed Bowing, his lips turned back in a sneer of contemptuous malignance. Dawlish had rarely seen so much expression put into a glance. 'If that little tyke is Bowing,' said

Ketch, 'and you believe anything he says, you're a mug.' He leaned forward and poured himself another drink, drank half of it and then said: 'What do you want?'

'Let's get one thing quite clear,' said Dawlish. 'I am backing Bowing.'

'The more fool you.'

'It could be,' admitted Dawlish. 'The point is that if it has to be a decision between the two of you, I would not choose you. I don't like anything about you, Ketch, or about your friends. What did you use at Brittling Hotel? Nitro-glycerine, or T.N.T.?'

Ketch said: 'I'm not wasting time talking to you, and if I have any more nonsense I'll call the police.'

'Oh,' said Dawlish, 'that will be interesting, for you see I am a policeman.'

Ketch's sudden look of astonishment held fear, while the other uttered an ugly expletive. Dawlish said sharply: 'Now listen to me. Two of your men have been detained, and have admitted being sent by you to a house near Woking with intent to injure and abduct. A serious charge.'

'It's ruddy nonsense!'

'One of them admits to being a party to the destruction of the Brittling Hotel, and was seen to come here after working on the gas-main at the hotel. There's a pretty strong chain of evidence which you won't find easy to break.'

'There's not a word of truth in it!'

'Oh, I think there is, quite a few words,' said Dawlish blandly. 'I don't like liars, and I'm not orthodox in my endeavour to get at the truth. In fact, that's why I'm used by the police, I can get away with so many things which they can't.'

'I—'

'Now don't interrupt,' chided Dawlish. 'I'm not particularly interested in the little men like you, Ketch, I'm after the Lord

Chief Justice himself. If you talk truthfully and to the point, you might be saved from police interrogation and a very long sentence. Remembering, of course, that they shoot spies.'

Ketch muttered: 'I don't know what you're talking about.'

'Why don't you bash his face in?' demanded Bowing heatedly.

Ketch ignored him, casting a furious look at Dawlish.

'You're no more a policeman than I am,' he snapped. 'I'm not such a fool as I look.'

'I hardly thought you could be,' said Dawlish unkindly.

He expected the two men to make an attempt to improve their position, but either they lacked the courage or had decided that the moment was not yet ripe. He was in something of a quandary. Obviously he needed to search the flat, equally obviously it might prove a waste of time. It was a rendezvous, certainly, but there was nothing to indicate that it was Ketch's home, or the depository of his private papers.

Having established the fact that they were afraid of the police, he did not mind whether they believed him a policeman or not, and his greatest concern was to get results without having to call upon Trivett for help. The more he saw of the affair the more he agreed, with Bowing, that if the police knew just what was happening, Sir Albert Clay would be warned: and a warning would almost certainly enable a plausible and convincing denial to be put up. True, Bowing might be wrong, and Clay quite innocent, but Dawlish imagined that Ketch's protested ignorance of the name had been a poor attempt at bluff.

He wished that he had Cunningham with him, or, better still, one or two of his friends who were more used to escapades of this sort.

'I've had enough of this,' said Ketch suddenly, and leaned forward towards the whisky bottle. Grabbing the neck, he raised the bottle and threw it at Dawlish.

Dawlish dodged to one side, but shot out a hand and caught the bottle in mid-air. Before Ketch could move, it was on the way back. Gasping with pain, and drenched with descending liquor, Ketch jumped to his feet.

At the same moment the other man dived for the door.

Dawlish swung round to stop him, but Bowing had already launched himself at the other's chin. The blow sent the man reeling backwards, to thud against the wall and fall heavily to the ground.

Bowing rubbed his knuckles and regarded Dawlish eagerly.

'Was that all right?'

'It was in the top flight,' Dawlish congratulated him warmly.

By then he was standing in front of Ketch. He could see that the encounter with the whisky had reduced him to a state which no threats could have done.

Dawlish yanked him up by his coat, and bundled him towards the door, then on to the bathroom. He filled a hand-basin, and pushed the man's face into the water. Ketch came up gasping, but it was obvious that the immersion had washed the spirit from his eyes.

Dawlish took a towel from a rail and tossed it towards him.

'That's the kind of thing that happens when you start playing fancy tricks,' he said, 'and the next time the consequences could be a lot worse. Hasn't it yet sunk into your mind that I'm serious, and that Dibben and Cromarty have talked?'

'So what?' muttered Ketch.

'Could it also sink in that unless you do the same you'll be charged on the strength of their statements?' demanded Dawlish.

'You—you're not a policeman.'

'I'm as near one as will make no difference to you.'

'I—I can't talk,' muttered Ketch. 'I tell you I daren't!' For the first time Dawlish believed the man. 'I—I'm only the go-between,' Ketch added.

'Between whom?' demanded Dawlish.

At that moment he thought that the man would talk. He was even wondering what fresh statement would be forthcoming, whether it would lead direct to Clay, and thus bring the affair to an abrupt end, when he heard a cry from the other room.

'Captain!' shouted Bowing. '*Captain!*'

There was a frenzied note in his voice, although he retained enough self-possession not to use Dawlish's name. For a moment Dawlish hesitated, seeing the glint in Ketch's eye. He glanced about the little bathroom. There was only a small window, not large enough for a man to get through. He would take a chance. Hurrying out of the bathroom, he snatched the key from the inside of the door, slamming the latter, and locking it.

Bowing's voice was still raised in frenzied appeal as he plunged into the other room.

Bowing was leaning perilously out of the window. Whether because he was being pulled or was trying to prevent the other man from getting away, Dawlish could not judge.

Dawlish reached the window in four long strides.

'Captain,' called Bowing faintly. 'I can't hold on, I can't hold on!'

Dawlish gripped his coat.

As he did so Bowing's feet left the floor, and he seemed to topple outwards. The weight on Dawlish's arm became much greater than he had expected, and the coat slipped from his grasp. He shot out his other hand just in time to prevent the youngster from falling, but by then he had lost his own balance. He felt himself being dragged slowly through the window in the wake of Bowing.

CHAPTER NINE

EXIT FROM CROMWELL ROAD

There followed a bad moment for Dawlish.

His left hand was clutching the window-ledge, but slipping, and the weight continued to drag him downwards. If he took his right hand from Bowing, the youngster would fall. Dawlish was not sure how far it was to the ground, but the rooms had high ceilings, and two floors would certainly mean a nasty fall.

The slow-motion effect of it gave him time to both think and manoeuvre. He edged himself towards the side of the window, so that he could get more support by pressing himself against it, and thus slow down the rate of progress still further. The light was shining into the street, showing a lamp-post with a small car standing nearby. It reflected on the blacked-out windows of the houses opposite. A stentorian voice bellowed:

'Put that light out!'

Bowing had stopped calling out. Dawlish, peering beyond him, saw that the youth was gripping the wrists of Ketch's companion.

'Put that ruddy light out!' the stentorian voice bellowed again.

Dawlish groped about with his right foot, and touched the

end of the settee. He jammed his foot against it and risked removing his grip on the window ledge. With both hands free to clutch Bowing, he strained backwards horribly aware that if his foot slipped all three would fall to the ground.

Suddenly the weight lessened.

He could not see what happened, but heard a cry, then a thud and a gasp which seemed like that of a man in pain. Fast upon it came a startled:

'Here, what's this?'

Presumably the warden was now beneath the window. Presumably too, Ketch's companion had slipped from Bowing's grasp. Vaguely Dawlish comprehended those things, then concentrated on pulling Bowing back into the room.

The blood had gone to the youngster's face, his hair stood on end and he was gasping for breath. He swayed drunkenly and would have fallen had not Dawlish guided him to the settee.

A shrill police whistle cut through the air.

'This isn't so good,' Dawlish murmured.

Quickly he left Bowing, and hurried down the stairs. Footsteps were approaching from outside, and a torch-light shone on the frosted glass panels of the front door. A heavy knock followed, as a sharp voice demanded:

'Is anyone there?'

'If only you knew,' muttered Dawlish.

There was little doubt that the rest of the tenants of the flats of 912A Cromwell Road would soon be disturbed, for the knocking reverberated through the whole building. Silently bolting the door, Dawlish raced up the stairs again, making for the bathroom of Cromarty's flat.

Ketch was bathing his eyes. Relief that he was still there, and awareness of the urgency of the position, sharpened Dawlish's voice. He said quietly:

'The police are here. If you've any sense you'll come with me and keep quiet.'

'Pol-*ice!*' gasped Ketch.

Dawlish grabbed the unprotesting man's arm and hurried him back to the sitting-room. Downstairs the thunderous knocking was getting louder, and there were footsteps on the stairs; it was evident that the residents of the other flats were on the move.

'Can you walk?' Dawlish asked Bowing quickly.

'I—I expect so.'

'Then get moving,' said Dawlish urgently. 'They'll be at the back door in a few moments.'

He gripped Ketch's elbow with one hand and Bowing's with the other, and hurried them through the kitchen to the fire escape outside the back door. He took his torch from his pocket, and pushed it into Bowing's hand.

'Keep that steady, and get down there,' he said.

Bowing gulped, and started moving unsteadily down the iron staircase. Shouts beneath them gave evidence that the little party had been seen.

Until then Ketch had behaved well, but when be reached the ground he twisted viciously in Dawlish's grasp. In a second he was free, and running madly.

'He's gone!' gasped Bowing.

'He's asked for it,' said Dawlish.

He hesitated, not knowing whether to follow Ketch or to look for an alleyway which would take him farther from the approaching police. In that moment of indecision he felt only luck could help them. Then Bowing gasped:

'F-follow me, Captain.'

The youngster had recovered well, and began to walk forward swiftly. They stumbled along a courtyard, then Bowing fumbled with the handle of a small gate. Ketch's footsteps would still be heard, as could those of his pursuers. Not only that: they raced past the gate to which Bowing had led Dawlish, and the two crouched down, hidden beneath the wall.

Three men in all went past.

'They'll catch Ketch,' muttered Bowing.

'That won't do anyone much harm,' said Dawlish, as Bowing opened the gate.

They stepped cautiously through, and on into a narrow passage. With every step Dawlish's confidence increased, for he believed that Ketch's escape had drawn off the police. In a few minutes they found themselves stepping cautiously into Cromwell Road.

It was deserted, but they could see, a hundred yards or so farther on, a gathering of torches, shapes and cars. Dawlish thought that one of the cars was an ambulance.

They were in the shadows, and safe enough from observation. Presently Dawlish thought it safe enough to move on. Endeavouring to subdue Bowing's agitated walk to a casual saunter he made for the West End.

They had covered at least half a mile before a taxi came in sight, but it passed them, ignoring their signal.

'We'll have to walk,' said Bowing resignedly. 'Strewth, am I tired!'

'Well, what happened?'

'It sounds idiotic to be fooled so easily,' said Bowing with a certain pride, 'but he threw a book at me. By the time I'd turned, he'd got the window open, and started climbing out. I shouted for you, and grabbed him.' There was a pause before Bowing added: 'I wonder if he broke his neck?'

Dawlish said dryly:

'You don't sound as if it would upset you all that much.'

'Upset me!' exclaimed Bowing. 'I'd like to think that all of them would be dead by the morning. It would save me and the others a lot of trouble!'

'Ye-es,' admitted Dawlish. 'But it might cause more.'

They walked in silence for some minutes, and then Bowing said:

'Captain Dawlish—you do believe me, don't you?'

Dawlish said quietly, 'I can't grant you Clay, yet, but you've struck something.'

'And you'll go on helping? You won't tell the police?'

'We'll have a talk about that some time. For the moment I agree that it's better for the police not to know. I won't let you down, old chap,' Dawlish added, and after a pause Bowing said gratefully:

'I know you won't. Thanks awfully.'

By then they were outside the flat. Dawlish, cautious by habit, kept a hand on his gun until he was turning the key in the lock, but there was no attempt to attack them either from inside or outside the flat. There was a light burning in one of the rooms, and he imagined that Felicity had decided to stay up.

Before he touched the handle of the door, a man's voice said:

'*Must* you keep doing that?'

Bowing went rigid, clutching Dawlish's arm. Dawlish stopped still, his heart beating fast.

Felicity said something, and then the man's voice responded. 'Does he often keep you up like this?'

Dawlish flung the door open with an exclamation of delight. 'By all that's holy and wonderful, Ted!'

Bowing stared in bewilderment as a man almost as big as Dawlish leapt up from the settee, his face creased in an expression of pure delight.

'Well, well,' said Dawlish with feeling, 'I haven't seen a better sight for years—always excepting Felicity.' He smiled down at her. 'But I'd forgotten. Ted, meet Mr Richard Bowing, a promising recruit. Bowing, this is Captain Edward Beresford. Your friend on the *Echo* may have mentioned him.'

'B-Beresford!' exclaimed Bowing.

His eyes glowed as he stretched out a hand, which Beresford took, engulfed and released.

'I've been hearing something about you,' said Beresford. 'And I'm all set to hear some more.'

'All in good time,' said Dawlish. 'Gosh, could I do with a drink!' He glanced at Bowing. 'You'll have one?'

'Er—I don't mind if I do,' said Bowing.

'You don't mind if you do!' exclaimed Beresford. 'I should say you don't. This is a rare privilege. Dawlish doesn't often take out his sample bottles.'

'Captain Beresford's little joke,' said Dawlish with a grin. 'It's his way of saying that he doesn't think that one bottle will be enough.' For a moment there was the clink and gurgle of bottles and glasses. Then they all sat back with evident enjoyment.

'This beer's not bad,' admitted Beresford. 'Now, what's to do?'

'How much leave have you got?' countered Dawlish.

'Not a day,' said Beresford, 'not even an hour. I'm on special duties.'

'Oh, blast it,' said Dawlish, 'I've a job on hand, and you'd be the very man for it!'

For they had worked together before. In fact, there had been no single escapade of Dawlish's in which Beresford had not taken a part. Until a few months before he had been with Dawlish in the Intelligence Department, complaining like Dawlish of having too little to do. Then he had been attached to a field unit, and sent to the West Country. Twice he had managed to get to London for short week-ends, and the last time had said that he expected to be on embarkation leave within a few weeks.

'Oh, well,' said Dawlish, a little bitterly, 'I suppose it can't be helped.'

'But suppose it *can*,' said Beresford, with a rather overdone solemnity, which, unable to keep up, he quickly abandoned. 'The thing is, my hearty, that the special duties have to do with you. I've been attached to you for the next week, and any extended period as may be necessary. What do you think about that?'

CHAPTER TEN

MORE MYSTERY

'Attached to me,' echoed Dawlish faintly.

'That's what I said,' Beresford assured him. 'You must know about it, surely?'

'I haven't the foggiest notion of what it's about,' said Dawlish bewilderedly. 'Attached to—'

'No, don't say it again,' implored Beresford. 'You'll be sending Bowing to sleep, he looks tired out as it is.'

Bowing's eyes were red-rimmed with fatigue, but they were bright enough, shining now with an intensity of excitement and hero-worship.

Dawlish looked thoughtfully at his friend.

'Did they give you any details?'

'None at all,' Beresford assured him. 'The C.O. merely informed me that I'd been detailed for special service, and was to report to you, here, as soon as possible. So I took the first train. I thought'—in turn Beresford himself looked puzzled—'I thought you'd made a request of some kind, and that something was brewing.'

'Something's brewing, all right,' admitted Dawlish, 'but I don't see that it's necessarily connected with this.' Deep in thought he paused, and then went on: 'Bowing and I have had quite a time.'

Briefly he told them what had happened. 'How I wish I had been there,' said Beresford regretfully, 'I could at least have stopped Ketch from escaping.'

'I'm not sure that he did,' said Dawlish. 'I think it's more than possible that the police caught him.'

'Did he recognize you?' Felicity asked quickly.

'He could give my description, and if he does, Trivett isn't likely to think I'm someone else,' admitted Dawlish. 'If he talks—' He shrugged and turned to Bowing. 'That is what I was coming to. If Ketch *has* talked and implicated you, the whole story ought to be told to the police.'

Bowing stared at him for a long moment. The flat was very quiet, as the others silently eyed the youngster. He swallowed hard, and his voice was unnaturally high when at last he spoke.

'I don't see why, Captain Dawlish. I mean, there's no reason why I shouldn't be arrested, is there? Ketch won't give anything away that matters, and I needn't talk. I mean, they won't arrest *you*,' Bowing added earnestly, 'and if you're still able to keep busy, it doesn't matter what happens to me.'

The sincerity of the words robbed them of any suggestion of bravado. Dawlish smiled a little.

'Oh well, we may not get to that stage. You'll have to leave it to me to handle things the best way I can, and if half a story for the police will satisfy them, half it will be.'

'I can't ask for more than that,' said Bowing.

The conversation for the next ten minutes was desultory, and then Felicity declared that it was time for bed.

The girls were occupying two small bedrooms, while a larger one with twin beds would have to accommodate the two men and Bowing. Bowing said at once that he would sleep in a chair, but the suggestion was vetoed, and a compromise made by inflating a Lilo and making it up as an additional bed in the double room.

Within half an hour all of them were asleep.

Before retiring, Dawlish had made sure that the doors were locked and bolted, and the windows secure. He did not seriously expect any attempt to break into the house, but the possibility was undoubtedly there. As he was going to sleep, he thought of Cunningham, McFee and the others at the cottage near Woking, but decided not to telephone them until the morning.

Dawlish was awakened soon after eight o'clock.

Felicity, in dressing-gown and slippers, was manoeuvring a tray of early-morning tea through the door. For a moment he lay and watched her, delighting in her prettiness and charm, before springing up.

Together they lowered the tray to the dressing-table without waking either Beresford or Bowing.

She glanced at both of them with an indulgent grin, then started to pour out.

At the clatter of cups, first Beresford, and then Bowing, turned over, grunted and finally sat up.

She left them with an airy wave of her hand and strict instructions not to hog the bathroom.

Dawlish, over a second cup of tea, was mulling over the fact that Beresford had been told to report to him for special duty.

Often in the past, when the affairs had been of an official or semi-official character, he had made urgent representations for Ted and for Tim Jeremy to help him, and this had been conceded. But he could not understand why Ted had been detailed this time. There was nothing official in what he was doing, and in due course he came to the conclusion that something else was brewing, about which he had not yet received his orders.

'And if that's so, it could make things sticky,' he decided. 'I wonder what time Whitehead will be up?'

Colonel Whitehead, the bland gentleman who was Dawlish's O.C., would not be at the office until ten o'clock, but he might be working at his flat, only a short distance from Dawlish's, before then. Dawlish decided it was worth a try, and leaving Felicity and Joan to prepare breakfast, nipped along the street. Reaching Whitehead's house, he was halted by a powerful '*View hallo!*'

He turned at once.

Coming towards him was a tall, thin man, whom he recognized immediately. He stood and stared, hardly able to credit that it was Tim Jeremy, for Tim should have been in the North of England. From somewhere he had obtained a bicycle. He was in uniform, and cycling at speed, drew up alongside Dawlish, grinning widely.

'Heaven help me,' said Dawlish faintly. 'I'm still dreaming. You've been told to report to me for special duties. Say it.'

'Well, you ought to know,' said Jeremy comfortably.

'That's just the trouble,' said Dawlish. 'I ought to know, but I don't. Tim, go along to Felicity, you'll find Ted with her. Break the news to them gently, and watch the effect. They'll tell you what's happened to date. I want to find out more from Whitehead.'

With an airy wave of his hand, which all but unseated him, Jeremy cycled away, while Dawlish, very thoughtfully, knocked at Whitehead's door.

He was admitted immediately, and after a short wait shown into Colonel Whitehead's study.

The Colonel was sitting at a large desk, with an untidy heap of papers in front of him. He was a biggish man, with drooping eyes which always held a smile, as if he could see a joke where other men could not. His urbane manner and soothing, mellow voice were well-known at Whitehall, while there were many who criticized the parties which he held at the Audeley Street house. That those parties were to do with espionage, that there, gathered at the Colonel's residence, were an amazing number of people returning from Occupied Europe with information they could pass on to the Colonel, was known to very few. Dawlish had no part in espionage abroad, his work dealt with activities in England: his especial concern being Fifth Columnists.

Whitehead smiled at him urbanely.

'I thought you were on leave, Dawlish. Pull up a chair, and sit down.'

'Thanks,' said Dawlish. 'I thought I was on leave, too.'

Whitehead raised his eyebrows inquiringly.

'Don't tell me that you've no idea what's been happening,' implored Dawlish, sitting down and accepting a cigarette. 'Thank you, sir. Beresford and Jeremy have just come to tell me that they've been ordered to report to me for special duties, but they don't know anything more than I do about the job.'

'Oh,' said Whitehead blandly, 'I don't know a great deal myself, except—' He leaned back in his chair, and added quietly: 'How have you been spending the last day or two, Dawlish? Amusing yourself?'

'More or less,' said Dawlish.

It was obvious that Whitehead knew something. But what? Dawlish felt a little uneasy. He had imagined that by outwitting Trivett he had made sure that no one knew just what he was doing, but Whitehead's 'amusing yourself' had shaken him.

'With the interesting Mr Bowing, I'm told,' said Whitehead.

'Well, yes,' said Dawlish. 'How did you hear of him?'

Whitehead began to sort through the papers on his desk. He unearthed a typewritten letter and handed it towards Dawlish.

Brief, and very much to the point, it was addressed to Whitehead, and written on a sheet of Home Office paper.

Dawlish wondered why he had not seen it before, and still more why Bowing had not mentioned it to him. He read:

Dear Sir,

This is to inform you that I can lodge information of very great importance if you will be good enough to grant me an interview, with yourself or with Captain Dawlish. Please don't ignore this letter.

Yours truly,

R. A. Bowing

'Well, well,' said Dawlish, and glanced at the date. It was January the 21st. 'I was up North at the time. Did you see him?'

'No,' said Whitehead. 'I wrote to tell him to come here, but he didn't turn up. I made some inquiries about the young man, and learned that he was no longer with the Home Office but had been fined for making a fool of himself.' Whitehead's expression was unreadable. 'I could have let it pass at that, but I thought it would be worth while getting further details. Here is the full *dossier*,' he added.

A little at a loss Dawlish took a sealed envelope from the Colonel's outstretched hand. 'This is getting beyond me,' he admitted. 'I'd no idea that he'd tried this way.'

'Perhaps I should have told you, since you were mentioned,' said Whitehead, 'but I discovered that Bowing had an acquaintance on the staff of the *Echo*, an indiscreet cub-reporter who told him where you were working, and that I was in charge. The reporter was reprimanded, and I put a man on to Bowing.'

'Who?' asked Dawlish.

'Parmitter. He didn't find out a great deal, except that a number of people from the Home Office—most of them no longer working there—were living at the same hotel as Bowing. Inquiries at the Home Office—I saw Mortimer Fraser myself—made it clear that Bowing and some of his friends had tried to interest Fraser in somewhat wild accusations against an anonymous member of the staff. D'you know Fraser?'

'Not yet,' admitted Dawlish.

Whitehead smiled. 'Well, the inquiries pointed to the possibility that Bowing and his remarkable gallery of friends were in fact an organization ready to trade with the Nazis.'

Dawlish said slowly:

'Are you sure of that?'

'My dear Dawlish, I haven't had time to be sure about anything,' Whitehead told him. 'The hints and suggestions that Bowing was working against the interest of the country were all very vague, and we couldn't persuade anyone to make positive accusations, but that was the trend of them. For my part, I couldn't see Bowing being the leader of anything more than a half-baked gang of melodramatic asses. Still, he was watched, and it grew apparent that he and his friends were frightened. Many of them had been attacked from time to time, and I came to the conclusion that when Bowing had been found guilty of attempting suicide—which was what it amounted to—he had been wrongly judged. Interesting, you'll agree?'

'Interesting is one word,' said Dawlish.

He felt bemused, for he was hearing Bowing's story from an entirely different angle. He was not surprised that news of it had failed to reach him, for Parmitter worked in a different office, and in direct connection with the Home Office. Moreover, Parmitter was a man very conscious of his position. Others under Whitehead's fatherly leadership might have confided in Dawlish, but no confidences could be expected from Parmitter.

'I was holding a watching brief on the affair when the hotel was blown up,' said Whitehead. 'Cunningham was seen to leave the scene, and to go to your flat. It was obvious that something was developing, and that whatever the truth of the matter, it needed attention quickly. So I sent for Jeremy and Beresford, and I had hoped to talk to you about it last night. I was detained at Downing Street,' continued Whitehead, 'and did not think it worthwhile calling you out at four o'clock. Bowing had been seen at the hotel, too, and he was later seen with you. Now that little mystery's cleared up!'

'Not altogether, sir, surely? There are still some odds and ends to be accounted for.'

'Just the kind that ought to appeal to you,' said Whitehead.

'Ye-es. Do the police know anything about this yet?'

'Certainly not. It's been handled with the utmost discretion. Bowing's letter infers that he had information about an official at the Home Office, and the inquiries we made were all off the record.'

'That was Bowing's idea, too,' said Dawlish.

He was thinking that his hope that Bowing had approached him quite unaware of his active concern in Fifth Column activities was gone. There was no coincidence at all. Through the garrulous indiscretions of a reporter, he had been known by Bowing to be interested in precisely that kind of work. Bowing, probably to try to shield the reporter, had pretended that he sought Dawlish's interest because of his reputation in other affairs.

'A promising young man, Mr Bowing,' conceded Whitehead. 'Are you on his side, Dawlish?'

'Provisionally,' said Dawlish slowly. 'There are some odd things I can't understand. He had the use of a cottage near Woking, complete with a sliding door and an emergency exit into the garden. That suggested money, but according to his story he and the others had very little to spare. I've been thinking about that,' he added slowly. 'Do you know about the place?'

'No,' said Whitehead. 'Tell me.' He looked at his watch, and shook his head in annoyance. 'By George, it's getting late. Have some breakfast with me, will you, and you can talk then.'

'Thanks very much,' said Dawlish. 'I'll telephone my flat first, if I may.'

'Of course,' said Whitehead, motioning to the telephone on his desk.

The Colonel went out to make arrangements for breakfast to be served for him and Dawlish, while Dawlish told Felicity enough to let her understand that Ted and Timothy were on the same mission. Everyone was at breakfast, he learned, but Bowing and Yvonne were not on speaking terms.

'A really happy family,' said Dawlish amiably. 'All right, my sweet, I'll be along as soon as I can.'

Over breakfast, he told Whitehead what had happened earlier.

'And the little French girl doesn't really fit in?'

'She doesn't,' admitted Dawlish, 'and after last night even less so. If I knew why she had insisted on returning to the cottage I'd be happier. All I can say is that she came back through a window, and then bumped into Dibben and Cromarty.' He shrugged his shoulders before adding: 'You've never come across the man Ketch, I suppose?'

'No,' said Whitehead. 'Now let me see—your chief problem is keeping your friend Trivett happy while giving nothing away.'

'Why shouldn't Trivett know?' asked Dawlish. 'He can be discreet enough, and he might be more useful if he knows just what I'm after.'

'Ye-es,' said Whitehead, helping himself to a piece of toast, 'but I'm not too happy about that. You know as well as I do that if any individual at the Home Office or elsewhere is suspected, the police can handle it as well as anyone. The trouble is that we're not sure who is suspected. You mention Clay. Bowing might be quite wrong, it *could* be Fraser.'

Dawlish nodded.

'Bowing has certainly jumped to conclusions,' Whitehead went on, 'but I think there might be something in it. He knows that the list was stolen, for instance. Of course, it's possible that he and the others are a subversive organization and that they're trying to escape the consequences by a show of frankness, but—'

'I doubt it,' said Dawlish. 'Some of the others may be in the racket, but Bowing's genuine enough.'

'Good. Well then, to get back to whether Trivett should know. He can't know from me, except through the Assistant Commissioner, and once the police start working on the case there are records, C.I.D. men activated and the whole gamut of the Yard set in motion. It would soon be obvious that they were watching someone, and that would be more than enough warning. At the moment I don't think anyone realizes that we're interested.'

Dawlish frowned thoughtfully.

'They can't be quite so dull as that, or they would be less worried about Bowing.'

'He's stirred up what trouble he could, and then been shot out,' said Whitehead. 'And these gentle hints are intended to fasten suspicion on him. The angle is: A youth of that type, these papers missing and other little spots of bother—oughtn't he to be thoroughly interrogated? No direct accusation, as I say, but hints from many places.'

'And you think that Clay, or whoever it is, is satisfied that we'll look for Bowing now?'

'More than that,' said Whitehead. 'I think that whoever it is believes that Bowing's bolt is shot and he can do no further harm.'

'Then why blow up the Brittling?' demanded Dawlish.

'For effect,' said Whitehead promptly, 'and to reduce the risks to the absolute minimum.'

'By ensuring that the police will be on the lookout for the perpetrators?' asked Dawlish with mild sarcasm. 'We can't stop the police doing that, after all. I don't know that we want to.'

He lapsed into silence, fully aware that Whitehead had said many things for the sole intention of stirring him to opposition and interest, and in fact he had done just that.

After a long pause, Whitehead asked:

'Can you make anything of it?'

'Why, yes,' said Dawlish, casually. 'That there's more to it than meets the eye hardly needs saying, sir, and you won't expect me to express any opinions at this stage.' He smiled. 'What I would like, if it can be arranged, is to tell the police half the story, and thus be able to call on their co-operation when necessary.'

'And by "the police" you really mean "just Trivett",' said Whitehead, pulling at the lobe of his ear. 'Well, provided he isn't told too much, that's all right.'

'Thanks,' said Dawlish. 'Is there anything else, sir?'

'I see you've been struck suddenly by an idea,' said Whitehead. 'But it's no use trying to make you formulate it, I suppose?'

'I couldn't if I tried,' said Dawlish earnestly. 'Before I go, sir, there is one thing. Apart from Sir Alfred Clay, is there anyone else whom you, personally, suspect?'

'No,' said Whitehead. 'All I know is that there have been leakages from the Home Office. Someone is playing a pretty deep game, Dawlish, and I trust you to put all you've got into it. You can, of course, take your leave after it's over.'

Dawlish left Whitehead's flat in a thoughtful mood. He was quite sure that Whitehead knew more, or at least suspected more than he had told him. He fancied that he understood the

Chief's reason, and when he reached his own flat he felt even more convinced of this.

Beresford and Jeremy were in his bedroom.

Dawlish went in and closed the door.

'Well?' asked Beresford promptly.

'An odd show,' said Dawlish, smoothing down his hair. 'The Old Man's mysterious about it, and I fancy there's been some trouble. Parmitter's been handling the job up to now.'

Beresford wrinkled his nose, knowing Parmitter well. 'I suppose he's muffed the job, and it's been pushed on to you.'

'That's what it looks like,' said Dawlish. 'The Old Man wouldn't let him down, of course, but he dropped the name into the conversation and left me to reach my own conclusions. He seems pretty sure that Parmitter hasn't given much away, while there's certainly bother at the Home Office. Whitehead hasn't really said what. You've passed on what you know, I suppose?' he added to Beresford.

The big man nodded, and Tim said:

'Yes, I'm up to date. What have we got, a *carte blanche*?'

'Very nearly, though I fancy they're still not being entirely open with us.' He shrugged his shoulders. 'We're in deep enough, anyhow. Do you feel energetic?'

'I do and I don't,' said Ted. 'Depends what's afoot.'

'What's the opening gambit?' Tim asked. 'Ketch?'

'No, he's my bird for the time being,' said Dawlish. I'd like you both, and Bowing, to go to Course Cottage and have a good look around. After that, go to McFee's place and find out whether Andy's all right, or whether they've had any bother. I think we'd have heard if anything had happened, but we'd better be sure. How much petrol have you got in the bus, Ted?'

'Enough for a hundred miles or so. What about Yvonne?'

Dawlish frowned.

'There's always one question we can't answer,' he said thoughtfully, 'and this time it's Yvonne. I think we'll leave her alone for a bit. She might decide to confide in Felicity, or even Joan. Is she still on bad terms with Bowing?'

'She's thawed out a bit,' said Beresford, 'but they're not bosom friends.' He straightened his tie. 'Well, off we go.'

Dawlish watched the three of them walking along the road, and then turned to smile at Felicity and Yvonne. Yvonne looked pale and worried, and he was sure that there was something on her mind, but decided that it would be best not to force her confidence.

He kissed Felicity goodbye, saying he was off to see Trivett.

But although he left the flat, he did not go to Scotland Yard. Instead, he stopped at the foot of the stairs, seeing a taxi pull up outside and a man step out.

It was Ketch.

CHAPTER ELEVEN

YVONNE IS PERSUADED

There were two choices open to Dawlish. He could go forward and meet the man, or move into the shadow of a door of one of the ground-floor flats. He chose the latter, and Ketch walked straight to the stairs, looking neither right nor left.

Dawlish waited until he had reached the landing, and then followed. A door opened, and Felicity's voice wafted down to him in brief inquiry. Then Ketch's.

'Have I the pleasure of speaking to Miss Deverall?' Dawlish could imagine the man's eyes kindling at the sight of Felicity: Ketch would almost certainly consider himself to be a ladies' man.

'Is Captain Dawlish in, by any chance?'

'I'm afraid not.'

'What a pity,' exclaimed Ketch. 'My name is Cartwright, and I was so anxious to see him. Is he likely to be long, do you know?'

'I've no idea,' said Felicity. 'If you care to leave a message I will see that he gets it.'

'No-o,' said Ketch hesitantly. 'I don't think I'll worry about that. I'll just leave my card, and you might be good enough to tell him that I called.'

As he spoke the man put his hand to his breast-pocket. Dawlish saw the movement. He was not surprised at the next, for even from the rear Ketch's attitude changed and his voice altered:

'*Don't make a sound!*'

Felicity stayed absolutely still.

'Get inside,' Ketch whispered.

Dawlish waited, without moving, until Ketch went into the flat. If Felicity saw the top of Dawlish's head beneath the banisters she made no sign. The door closed, and silence descended.

Dawlish leapt quickly up the stairs.

He was puzzled, and at the same time angry with himself. He had taken too much for granted in assuming that he would not be identified, and that the flat was not in any danger. It angered him to think that he had left Felicity in a spot, and that if he had gone out five minutes earlier Ketch would have had little difficulty in getting whatever he wanted.

Very quietly Dawlish inserted his key into the lock and turned it. The door opened without a sound. The hall was empty. In the doorway of the lounge Felicity was standing, facing Ketch, now openly flourishing a gun.

'Get inside, blast you!' rasped Ketch.

Something had angered him, and the suavity of his earlier manner had completely gone. Felicity backed away, tight-lipped. Ketch followed. Suddenly his voice rose in triumph.

'*Got* you!'

In that moment Dawlish nearly gave his presence away. He stopped himself in time, however, hearing a gasp from Yvonne, realizing for the first time that it was for Yvonne Ketch had come.

'You thought you'd dodged me, did you,' Ketch went on, his voice harsh and menacing. 'But you can't get away from me as easy as that. You're coming with me, and this time you won't get away.'

Felicity said: 'She's staying here.'

Ketch snapped: 'If I have another word out of you I'll bash your pretty face in. What would Dawlish say about that? If you want to be safe, shut up.' To Yvonne he said: 'Get your coat on.'

Dawlish heard a movement, and then Felicity said:

'Yvonne, stay where you are.'

By then Dawlish was just on the threshold. He could not see Yvonne, who was hidden behind the door, but he did see Felicity back quickly away. Ketch struck at her, his face taut with fury.

'Now what's it all about?' asked Dawlish gently.

Ketch swung round, raising his gun. Dawlish moved swiftly to one side, and a bullet, from a silenced automatic, buried itself in the wall. In the same movement Dawlish swept his hand upward, striking Ketch's forearm and sending the gun flying. Ketch licked his lips, his confidence gone as swiftly as it had left him on the previous night.

At first Dawlish had been furiously angry, as much with himself as with Ketch, but now he was more composed. No harm had been done, and Ketch had delivered himself into his hands; this second opportunity must not be missed.

Ketch muttered:

'You'd better be careful.'

'Of what?' asked Dawlish, genuinely curious.

'You know what of,' snapped Ketch, his confidence returning. 'You're going to get what you don't expect if you butt in any more.'

'I really think—'

'Never mind what you really think,' said Ketch. 'I've just come from the police, see. They caught me last night, and they thought they had something on me, but when I described *you* they realized that I was all right. They want you pretty bad, Dawlish, and I can identify you. If you try to be clever, I'll tell them just what they want to know. *You* killed Vic, that's a murder rap.' Ketch leaned forward, his expression villainous.

But Dawlish was not thinking of expressions, only of the news which he believed to be genuine enough. He had thought that Ketch had been caught the previous night, and was not really surprised that the man had been released. But the news that 'Vic' had been killed in the fall was of greater importance. But for the interview with Whitehead he would have been in difficulties. As it was, Ketch imagined that he held the upper hand.

He might as well continue to think so, mused Dawlish, eyeing the man with detachment. The silence encouraged Ketch. He went on:

'I didn't think it would take long to fix you, Dawlish. You big louts are all the same.'

Dawlish laughed.

'You can't laugh your way out of this,' snapped Ketch. 'I've come to take the French dame away, and that's what I'm going to do.'

Dawlish looked at Yvonne.

She was breathing quickly, and in her eyes there was a great appeal.

'Do you want to go with Mr Ketch?' asked Dawlish quietly.

'No, *mon dieu*, no!'

'Then you stay,' said Dawlish decisively. 'But while you're here, Ketch, we might as well find out why you want her.'

'If you don't keep your nose out of this, you know what'll happen to you.'

Swiftly Dawlish decided that it might be an advantage to let Ketch continue to believe that he was in danger from the police. He said sharply:

'Cut that out, Ketch. Bowing and I were at Cromwell Road last night; our evidence will cover yours.'

'I got in first,' said Ketch craftily, but his eyes darted to and fro as he grappled with this new idea. '*And* I gave a full story of how it happened. Never mind about that, I want the Frenchie.'

'We'd got as far as asking why,' said Dawlish.

'That's my business. See here, I'm not *playing* at this, I'm serious. You can go around being big brother to a little runt like Bowing if you like, but I'm in this for a big stake. The girl means nothing to you. Hand her over.'

Dawlish shook his head.

'I see that it's going to take a long time to make you see sense,' he commented. 'I told you last night that I'm not particularly interested in you, personally. But I want your leaders, Ketch.'

He stopped abruptly, for there was a ring at the front door.

Either the caller had made a very stealthy approach, or Dawlish had been so intent on a passage of words which seemed to be getting him nowhere that he had missed all sounds of approach. Cautiously, his hand about his gun, prepared for almost any contingency, he opened the door. Superintendent Trivett, well-groomed, debonair, faced him.

'Hallo, Pat,' he said in friendly enough fashion. 'Just going out?'

'Just waiting for you to come in,' said Dawlish, recovering quickly and putting as good a face on it as he could. 'I've had a visitor, Bill, who thinks he knows you. Don't be surprised if he gets excited.'

He broke off abruptly, for Ketch came running into the hall, a tense, desperate expression on his face. He pushed Dawlish off, kicked at Trivett's legs and then went rushing down the stairs.

When Dawlish reached the pavement Ketch was haring along the street, already too far off for any hope of recapture.

Dawlish turned, expecting to see Trivett immediately behind him. Instead, Trivett was running in the opposite direction. For a moment Dawlish thought that the policeman had made a mistake in direction, but then he saw Yvonne ahead of the policeman, running quite as desperately as Ketch had done.

Hesitating for only a moment Dawlish followed them. Spinning round a corner Yvonne was turning into a narrow street which led to a rabbit-warren of mews and alleys. Trivett was half-way across the road when a man seemed to appear from nowhere. There was no deliberate shouldering, but the two men collided and Trivett staggered back. So did the other fellow, but he kept his feet, while Trivett hit the road heavily. Dawlish, close behind them, had an impression that the man deliberately shot out a leg to impede him.

Dawlish jumped aside and ran on. By this time Yvonne appeared to be tiring. Another spurt of speed and Dawlish drew within a yard of her. He stretched out a hand and gripped her arm.

She was gasping for breath, as, indeed, he was himself. As they slowed down she muttered in an unsteady voice:

'Why—can't you leave—me alone?'

Dawlish patted her arm good-temperedly as they turned and began to walk back towards Audeley Street.

Trivett was limping towards them.

Silently he ranged himself on the other side of Yvonne.

'Did you get the chap who crashed you?' asked Dawlish.

'No,' said Trivett, obviously annoyed with himself, 'he got away. The fall shook me.'

'It shook the road,' said Dawlish with a sudden grin. 'But let's leave the chatter till we get to the flat.'

Trivett nodded, and they plodded along in silence. Felicity

was waiting for them in the hall. She came forward hurriedly, her concern for Yvonne, who looked as if she were likely to burst into tears at the slightest provocation.

'Look after her, Fel, will you?' asked Dawlish.

'Why must you keep me here? Why will you not let me go?' Yvonne uttered the words sharply, raising a clenched fist, but still looking woebegone and frightened. 'I need no looking after!'

'We aren't going to agree about that,' said Dawlish equably. 'The Superintendent and I need to talk for a few minutes, you go with Felicity and have a cup of tea. You'll feel ten times better.' He spoke as he would to a small child who was out of temper, and watched her good-humouredly as she walked dejectedly into the lounge, Felicity holding her elbow.

'The dining-room for us,' said Dawlish. 'Thirsty?'

'I could do with a drink,' admitted Trivett.

Dawlish busied himself with bottles and glasses for a few moments, then both men sank back into easy-chairs. Trivett accepted a cigarette, and then said grimly:

'What is it all about, Pat? Just what are you up to?'

'We-ell,' said Dawlish judiciously, 'I *think* I'm trying to help Yvonne and some friends of hers. It is possible, however, that you're going to be annoyed before the morning's out.'

'I'm annoyed as it is,' said Trivett sharply.

'This time you'll have good reason,' rejoined Dawlish smiling; but there was no answering smile in Trivett's eyes. His voice was stern when he spoke.

'Listen, Pat. You and I are good friends, and you can get away with a lot of things that others couldn't, but you know as well as I do that there are limits to what you can do on your own.'

'Don't I just!' admitted Dawlish ruefully. 'I suppose what you're really telling me is that a gentleman giving his name as

Cartwright lodged a complaint that I'd broken into his flat, and had something to do with the breaking of someone else's neck?'

Trivett stared at him.

'Are you admitting it?'

'Good Lord, no!' exclaimed Dawlish. 'But the same gentleman, calling himself Cartwright, but actually named Ketch, came to see me this morning and told me what he'd done. You saw him just now, and he didn't behave as if he wanted to try to brazen his story out, did he?'

'No,' conceded Trivett, 'but—'

'I know, I know,' said Dawlish. 'You've had a word with Assistant Commissioner Morely, and you've decided that I've got to tell you exactly what's been happening. Last night I would have called you justified, old man, for it's been an odd business and I couldn't confide. I can't now, but—'

He told the Superintendent something of what Whitehead had passed on to him, omitting only the venue of the inquiries. He knew that Trivett, as a policeman, would be disgruntled by the lack of confidence, but as a man would be prepared to admit that there might be cogent reasons for it. He made no interruptions, but when Dawlish had finished, said:

'I don't think a lot of it, but why did you put the cart before the horse? You knew something about it before you started to work for Yvonne.'

Dawlish registered a trick to himself: Trivett was satisfied that Yvonne, not Bowing, was the central character about whom the events of the night before had revolved.

'Nothing at all,' he assured the policeman, 'I took a chance, Bill, and it came off. For instance, do you know what really started me? After the lilies, and the rest of the business, I mean. Yvonne was staying at the Brittling Hotel last night—or rather yesterday afternoon. You know what happened to that place.'

He expected to create effect, and succeeded: it was one of the rare occasions when Trivett was out of countenance. The other recovered quickly, but his manner thereafter was sharper and grimmer. He knew that Dawlish would not quote Whitehead unless he had authority, and that in the peculiar conditions brought about by the war Whitehead could, and when necessary would, work independently of the police.

'Well, if that's what's been decided,' he said, repressively, 'there's nothing either of us can do about it. But is it Whitehead's fault that you've decided to boycott me—or is it yours?'

'Now, now, don't get het up,' protested Dawlish. 'Only by the most ardent pleading did I get permission to tell you anything about it, and I even went so far as to tell Whitehead that I'd like to give you the whole story, believing that you would treat it as unofficial, and keep it under your hat. Can you?'

Trivett eyed him thoughtfully, and then slowly shook his head.

'Not now, Pat.' His manner had relaxed, probably because he was no longer suspicious that Dawlish was deliberately crowding him out. 'Morely knows about the Brittling, and the show at Cromwell Road last night. I'll tell him that it was concerned with your Department, and he'll check up with Whitehead. If I'm not to know it officially I'd better not know anything about it at all. Yet,' he added hopefully.

'The day will dawn when we can tell the world about it,' said Dawlish. 'Meanwhile, here's a delicate point. Yvonne hasn't talked to you, and isn't likely to. But she's in the show somewhere, and might talk to me. I don't want to be awkward, but—'

'All right, all right, I'll go,' said Trivett.

He left a few minutes afterwards, with Dawlish's promise that he would not be kept in the dark a moment longer than was necessary.

When the door closed behind the policeman, Dawlish ran his hand through his hair with a certain desperation. True, he knew a little more than Trivett, but not so much more. Whitehead was keeping things back from him, just as he was doing from Trivett. A queer business; Dawlish was by no means sure that he liked it.

But Yvonne was his immediate concern.

Much of her tension had gone when he went into the lounge. Chatting in French to Felicity over tea and biscuits, about her experiences in Occupied France, she stopped abruptly as Dawlish entered.

'Hallo,' said Dawlish amiably. 'The policeman's gone.'

'Gone where?' demanded Yvonne.

'Back to his office,' Dawlish assured her. 'I've persuaded him that you are far more likely to confide in me than in him, and he's agreed to leave it to me.' He took a cup of tea from Felicity, and sat down, crossing his legs comfortably. 'It took some doing,' he declared, 'but we have a chance for a talk now, Yvonne. And you owe us something.'

'What is it I owe you?'

'We sent Ketch off at the double, and dispensed with the policeman,' said Dawlish. 'You're worried by them both, aren't you?' He took her silence for assent, and added: 'So is Bowing, and the rest of your friends.'

Yvonne drew a deep breath, and said emphatically:

'Friends? *They* are not my friends, I trust none of them!'

The words startled Felicity, and made Dawlish frown. He remembered hearing of the coolness between Bowing and Yvonne, but had paid little attention to it, thinking that it was because Yvonne had returned to Course Cottage, and thus offended Bowing, who would be quick to voice resentment. It had not occurred to him that the restraint had started with

Yvonne, and the vehemence of her words puzzled as well as surprised him.

'I thought you were trying to help them,' said Dawlish mildly.

'*Help* them!' she exclaimed. 'They were to help *me*, the cheats and traitors that they are! I told them too much, how else should Ketch know? One of them betrayed me—one, or all of them. Why else should I return to the house last night, except to find out who it was, or whether *you* were responsible for it?' She talked so swiftly that her words were difficult to understand, for although her choice of English was good she put the accent on the wrong syllables in her excitement—and certainly she was excited. 'Until yesterday, yes, I thought they were friends, but now—I wonder! And I wonder, also, whether they hate the Germans as I do, or whether they are traitors to their country as well as to me. How can I find that out? How can I tell whom to trust?'

She stopped abruptly, staring wide-eyed at Dawlish, her lips parted and unsteady.

CHAPTER TWELVE

AND YVONNE CONFIDES

Dawlish returned the French girl's gaze equably, trying not to reveal his sense of increasing excitement. He thought little about the doubts she cast upon Bowing and the others; that could come later. What he needed now was to hear her story, her part in what was happening.

'I'm helping all I can,' he said mildly.

'But you are a friend of Bowing's!'

'No more than of yours,' said Dawlish. 'Listen to me, Yvonne. I've had nothing to do with this until you tried to interest me. I advised you to go to the police, but apparently you won't confide in them, and I've had quite a job preventing them from putting you under arrest.' He saw her shrink back from his words, which he had deliberately exaggerated. 'But it has been done, they're prepared to leave it to me. They trust me.'

'Because they know you will tell them everything,' she said bitterly.

'Everything of importance, but only if it will help them to clear up the mystery,' said Dawlish. 'Yvonne, you're making yourself ill, you know. You're afraid of the police, and of Ketch, and now of Bowing. You seem to be alone in London, apart from those you no longer trust. That's neither good nor safe.'

'No,' said Yvonne in a small voice. 'I am alone, yes. Sometimes I feel that what I know will kill me, that I shall never see the end of worry and anxiety. These people are strangers, they do not know my country or my language. But you and Miss Deverall—'

She paused, but Dawlish said nothing. He wondered what manner of revelation could be forthcoming, could conceive of nothing likely to explain her fears, Ketch's interest in her, and also her nervousness of the authorities.

She said abruptly:

'To reach here from Spain, I killed three men. It is known to your police. They do not know my real name, they do not know that I am wanted by the Spanish authorities on a charge of murder. And it is a just charge, I killed them. If I tell all that I know, I must also tell that, and then I am lost.'

Dawlish saw the girl's expression and believed that she spoke the truth. For the first time he understood much of her anxiety. She said sharply:

'Why do you not say something?'

'We-ell,' said Dawlish, 'there isn't much to say, Yvonne. You killed three men who presumably wanted to keep you in Spain or send you back to France. Many people have been killed for a similar reason, it's part of the war.'

She swept the hair from her forehead, and he saw that her hand was unsteady. Presently she went on:

'I came from the Occupied zone, as I have said. I helped in the making of a newspaper which was spread about France secretly. I was suspected, and had to fly. I reached Spain, and there was apprehended. I was being taken back to France in a car, by three men. The car was climbing a steep hill. I stood up, and the driver slowed down quickly. I jumped out, and then seized a stone and struck the driver with it. He lost control of the car, and all three of them went over the precipice, they were killed like that.

'I did not think that I would be able to escape, but then I met friends who found me a small boat, and I was able to smuggle myself first on board a Portuguese ship and then an English one. How I did that does not matter, Captain Dawlish. What matters is that when I reached England I was Yvonne Lejeune, and had false papers to support that name. Yet all the time I remember those three men, and how I killed them. And when I was at the Home Office, being questioned, I saw a notice from Spain—it concerned the real me, Yvonne Dubonnet. The photograph on it was a poor one, and I was not recognized. Afterwards I was befriended by Miss Lancaster and the others, and I told them the truth. I wished to know what was on that paper from Spain.'

She stopped again, and then went on haltingly:

'They obtained a copy of it. I was required on a charge of murder, and it was decided by your authorities that I should be sent back to Spain. I was accused of having robbed the men, of being a thief and a murderess. I felt then that I could not tell the police everything. They would not believe what I have told you. It would be thought that I had lied in order to save myself. Is that not so?'

'It's possible,' conceded Dawlish.

'Then it was that I discovered what Bowing and the others were doing, or pretending to be doing, and so I joined them. I have helped, a great deal. I know German as well as Spanish and other languages, and some of the men who followed us spoke in foreign languages. I went with Bowing, to listen to what was said, and I have learnt a great deal, making notes of what I heard. One day I was seen. Bowing and I were known to have overheard a conversation. That was three days ago—and you know what has happened since. That is why Ketch was so anxious to get me, and'—her voice sank lower—'I heard Ketch talking, and he said that he knew why I was wanted in Spain, that I would not dare to go to the police. Only Bowing, and my *friends*'—she uttered that word bitterly—'could have told him of that. One of them, or all of them, betrayed me.'

She pressed both her hands against her forehead, and then added abruptly:

'And, now, I suppose, you will tell the police.'

'No,' said Dawlish. He smiled reassuringly. 'The thing of importance is your notebook.'

'I have that,' she said.

'Where?'

'Inside my clothes,' she told him. 'It was plain to me that the record of what had been said was of importance, though it seemed harmless enough to me.'

'We might read something into it,' said Dawlish. 'Will you give it to Felicity?'

'I will do that,' she said.

He left her, moving to the telephone. She had told the story in such detail that he did not think that it was false, though there were parts of it he could not understand. If it were true that the Home Office were prepared to arrange for her extradition, that would be all the proof he needed, and he wondered how quickly he could get the information. Frowning a little, he dialled Scotland Yard, and was soon connected with Trivett.

'Now I'm coming cap in hand,' said Dawlish without preamble. 'I want some information, Bill.'

'What is it?' demanded Trivett suspiciously.

'A list of extradition orders pending.'

Trivett did not answer immediately; there was little doubt that he would associate the request with Yvonne, and might identify her with Yvonne Dubonnet. But Trivett would play fair. His voice answered almost at once.

'I'll send a copy round.'

'Good man,' said Dawlish.

He replaced the receiver, lingering a little longer than necessary until he judged Yvonne had had time enough to get out the notebook.

When he re-entered the sitting-room she was showing it to Felicity. As the notes were in shortland, and in three different languages, they meant precisely nothing to her. Dawlish grinned spontaneously.

'It looks as if we'll need an expert for that.'

'I can transcribe it,' said Yvonne, 'if there is a typewriter.'

Dawlish dived into his bedroom and unearthed a portable machine. In a few minutes Yvonne was sitting at the dining-table, with paper and carbon-paper on one side, and the note-book on the other. She looked eager and much happier, and began to type with a speed which surprised Dawlish.

They left her alone with the door ajar.

'Will it help much?' Felicity asked quietly.

'It could do,' said Dawlish cautiously. 'Trivett's sending a list round, and we'll be able to check up on Yvonne Dubonnet. What do you make of her?'

'I think she's probably told the truth.'

'I'm going to get a nasty surprise if she hasn't,' admitted Dawlish. 'But it doesn't carry us much further along the main theme. I wish—'

He did not say what he wished, for the telephone rang.

There was an extension within reach, and he leaned forward and lifted the receiver.

'Dawlish, speaking.'

'Indeed? You surprise me,' said Ted Beresford with heavy

humour, 'I thought you were having forty winks. How are tricks?'

'Everything's quiet here,' Dawlish assured him.

'And everything's quiet here,' said Beresford repressively. 'This prize collection of nitwits is going through the most ghastly play you've ever heard in your life, and they're doing it in the wood-shed, if you please.'

'What about the two roughnecks?'

'Even they are being forced to listen,' said Beresford disgust-edly. 'Nothing else to relate. Andy's all right, and Tim's seeing some house agents in Woking.'

'Why house agents?'

'Because Course Cottage is in the market. Late owner recently deceased. At least four lots of people called to look over it while we were there.'

He broke off, mumbling something that sounded like: 'Half-a-mo.' There was a pause, before he spoke again: 'Tim's just coming up the garden path, do you want a word with him?'

'Yes,' said Dawlish. 'What kind of a place is McFee's cottage?'

'Oh, just a dump,' said Beresford. 'Something on seaside chalet lines, with plenty of ground. They used to do some poultry keeping, but the garden's pretty well derelict now. McFee's a surly customer.'

'What do you make of them generally?' demanded Dawlish.

'Odd show, as a matter of fact,' said Beresford. 'They all seem pretty het up. They've had about three quarrels in the last half-hour. I'm now in the little front room,' continued Beresford chattily. 'Tim's coming up the weed-grown path. He's frowning. He looks very hot. He's getting nearer. He's thrown a cigarette away. He's reached the front door, and he's knocking—wait just a moment, folk, and I'll hand the microphone over to my colleague!'

'Ass,' said Dawlish.

The pause before Jeremy came to the 'phone was short-lived, and with the first word Dawlish caught a hint of puzzlement in his friend's voice.

'You there, Pat? . . . here, I've struck a queer one.'

'What is it?' asked Dawlish.

'Course Cottage—Ted's told you it's on the market? . . . good. Well, the owner was a Mr Jeremiah Clay, who died a month or so ago, and his brother, Sir Alfred, is the sole executor. Odd, don't you think?'

'Odd!' exclaimed Dawlish. 'My oath, it's more than that, if Bowing and his brood had a free run of Clay's cottage. Where is Bowing?'

'In the woodshed.'

'Don't let him out of your sight,' said Dawlish urgently. 'We want that young man!'

There was an exclamation from Tim, and from someone farther away from the telephone a shout. Dawlish held on, his hand tight about the instrument. There were running footsteps, a mutter of voices and then Tim's voice, sharp and filled with urgency.

'The woodshed's on fire,' he said. 'It doesn't sound too good. I'll ring as soon as I can.'

He replaced the receiver, while Dawlish stood for a moment staring into space.

CHAPTER THIRTEEN

NOT MUCH LEFT

As he replaced the telephone, Tim Jeremy heard a shout from Beresford, and another, more distant, call from somewhere at the end of McFee's cottage garden.

Tim lifted the receiver again, and asked for the fire station. Quickly he gave such information as he had. The cottage was known as '*Orchards*', the fire had only just started but seemed of big proportions. Did the fireman know the place?

'Near the golf-course, isn't it?' the man said. 'That's all right, sir, thank you.'

Tim replaced the receiver again and hurried out through the front door. Rounding the house he was confronted by the woodshed, now a mass of flames and smoke.

As he drew nearer he felt the heat rolling in a mighty wave towards him, fanned by a steady wind. He could hear the roaring and the crackling, and see the long tongues of flame shooting up into the air. He could see Cunningham bent double as he carried something in his arms. He called out:

'How many inside?'

'Most—of 'em,' gasped Cunningham.

Both men plunged forward, but as they neared the burning mass, smoke and flames reached out at them, driving them back.

They could not get nearer, and for a moment were afraid that Beresford had been too late to get out. But they saw him staggering forward, an incredible sight, for Bowing was beneath one arm, and he was dragging Playfair with the other. McFee came reeling out behind him, his clothes alight. Tim rolled him on the ground to put out the flames. Cunningham had brought a girl, but there were no others in sight, and the flames were increasing, driving them farther back. By then the woman of the house had arrived, with a stirrup pump and two buckets of water, but they were of little use. One side of the shed was a mass of burning timbers, red-and-white-hot flakes were falling from it, while other, lighter pieces were flying into the air. Crackling and spitting, the dry wood had caught so fiercely that there was no chance to beat the flames.

Then, from nearby, came the clanging of a fire-engine.

It made its way alongside the chalet, drawing up not far from the woodshed. Blue-clad men of the Auxiliary Fire Service came running with hoses, others went to a hydrant and a heavily built man approached Tim and Cunningham.

'There isn't much left,' said Tim Jeremy hoarsely.

'Nasty affair,' said the A.F.S. leader. 'Everyone's out, I suppose?'

'I wish they were,' said Cunningham. 'I wish to God they were!'

The A.F.S. man said nothing, for obviously there was nothing he or anyone else could do. By then an ambulance and first-aid party had arrived. Of those who had been pulled out Bowing was least badly hurt, and first to recover consciousness. His clothes were torn and singed, much of his hair had been burned off, but he was able to stand up. Playfair, McFee and the girl were all unconscious, and of them the girl was the most badly burned.

Of the three men, only Beresford had been burned enough to need first-aid, and he refused to go to the post. All of their clothes had suffered, but none of them so severely that they needed a change before returning to London.

Their impotence, and the knowledge of the number of men and women who had died in the fire, made them unusually silent. Feeling helpless and useless they went into the kitchen and brewed tea, bringing it into the small front room. From the window they could see Bowing walking alongside an ambulance, in which the girl was being taken away. He watched from the gate as the ambulance went off, and then walked slowly and dejectedly back to the chalet. He accepted a cup of tea but seemed hardly aware of what he was doing.

Soon afterwards a car drew up outside the front gate.

By then there were only two or three firemen left to make sure that the embers did not start more outbreaks elsewhere, and a Red Cross nurse who was with the tenant in the kitchen. McFee, Playfair and May Larkin, the girl, had all gone to the local hospital.

Dawlish, stepping out of his car, one he had borrowed from Whitehead, saw the glowing ruin of the woodshed at once. He walked quietly towards the chalet, meeting Beresford, who took him into the small front room. Dawlish's eyes swept over Bowing, and the grim, pale faces of Cunningham and Jeremy. Until then he had had no idea of the seriousness of the fire, but was half-prepared for Bowing's sudden outburst.

'You see what's happened. I thought you were clever!'

'What has happened?' asked Dawlish quietly.

'What's happened? *What's happened?*' repeated Bowing in a tense voice. He stood up, his arms rigid by his sides, his hands clenched. There was a glitter in his eyes and tears seemed very close to the surface. 'You've the ruddy nerve to come here and ask what's happened! Why weren't you here? What the hell have you been doing? I'll tell you what's happened!' His voice, harsh and broken, echoed about the small room. 'All my friends have been killed, roasted alive, can you understand that? Burned alive, they only just got May out! Oh, my God, I can't bear it, I can't bear it!'

He raised his hands towards the ceiling, his face a ghastly pallor, his eyes twitching with a feverish glint.

'Phoebe—Rose—Charley—Meg—Robbie—oh, God!' He repeated the names again and again, then suddenly buried his face in his hands and began to cry.

There was nothing they could do, nothing Dawlish thought it was wise to do. He looked questioningly at Tim Jeremy, who told him in a low voice that only Bowing, McFee, Playfair and May Larkin had been rescued.

'Have the police been yet?' Dawlish asked.

'I haven't seen them.'

'They'll be along. How did it happen?' He looked at Andy Cunningham, knowing that Andy had been in the shed with the others. His face looked strangely different, for his hair was scorched and his eyebrows gone.

'I don't know altogether, Pat. I was in there, with the bunch. They were putting on this rehearsal. I'd loosened Dibben and Cromarty's gags, and they were making comments all through, barracking the players good and hard.' Cunningham paused, as if the scene remained vividly before him. 'There were three of them in the scene, Playfair, McFee and the girl Larkin. I was standing by the door. Suddenly it closed.'

The others stiffened. 'I felt the draught of its shutting, and turned to see what had happened,' Cunningham went on. 'I thought the wind had blown it to. There's a padlock and a bar on the outside, by the way, but nothing to fasten it inside.'

'Go on,' said Dawlish.

'I pushed at it,' said Beresford, 'but it wouldn't open. And then the place caught fire.' His voice cracked. 'Just like that. In an instant. Not in one place, but in half-a-dozen. There were sudden bursts of flame by the door, by the window, in the roof. The whole place was in a panic by then. I hurled myself at the door, and managed to get it open. I got the girl out, and then Beresford came up and collared Bowing and Playfair. McFee made it on his own, but the rest'—he paused for a moment, and then added in an expressionless voice: 'They hadn't a chance. It was more like an explosion than a fire, it simply caught the place and turned it into an inferno in a matter of seconds.'

Dawlish's eyes were half-closed, and he was looking towards Bowing. 'The woodshed had been prepared for something just like that, of course. It sounds like phosphorus-plus, spread about the place and starting off at a certain temperature. The wood must have been soaked in something too. Anyhow, the firemen Johnnies will give us some news of that.'

'*Prepared for it?* My oath!' exclaimed Tim Jeremy.

'Certainly there was nothing normal about it,' said Dawlish. 'Almost as certainly someone expected Bowing and his crowd to take refuge there after being pushed out of Course Cottage. Nice people, these! Were Bowing and McFee as much in danger as the others?'

'Every man jack of them,' said Cunningham.

'H'm. I—'

'What do you mean by that?' demanded Bowing thickly.

His smoke-streaked face turned towards Dawlish, and there was more than a suggestion of belligerence in his manner.

'Now take it easy,' said Dawlish. 'You did all that you or anyone could, and if you're on the square in this thing you've nothing with which to reproach yourself. If these three couldn't do anything about it, no one could.' He smoothed back his hair, and then regarded Tim Jeremy. 'We'll get off,' he said. 'You'd better wait and tell the police just what happened, Tim. All right with you?'

'Yes, I'll stay,' said Tim.

None of them reflected that Dawlish's suggestions were tantamount to orders, and that not one of the trio would seriously consider saying 'no'. Tight-lipped and red-eyed, Bowing went with them to the gate, and climbed into the Bentley. Tim watched them go off, and as they started, a police-car drew up with two uniformed men and a plain-clothes Inspector. Dawlish drove on, while Tim prepared to relate once again such details as he knew of the tragedy.

The drive to London was a fast one.

Dawlish drove as if he were anxious to gain every second, but he took no chances. In a little more than forty minutes they were outside the Audeley Street flat. They found Felicity and Yvonne upstairs, waiting for them.

He told them as briefly as he could what had happened, his eyes fixed on Yvonne.

He noted that she seemed much easier in manner. There was colour in her cheeks, and much of the tension she had shown earlier had disappeared. But as she listened to that grim recital, the tension returned.

Bowing said abruptly:

'And that's how much good *Dawlish* was.'

'Would it have been different had he not been helping?' Yvonne asked quietly. 'Did he suggest that place to hide?'

'What's that got to do with it?' muttered Bowing. 'What are you going to do now, Dawlish?' He had dropped the 'Captain', and his manner was both abrupt and challenging. 'Do you still think you can handle it yourself?'

'It wouldn't surprise me,' said Dawlish mildly. 'But first of all, there are some things to be worked out, Bowing. Yvonne tells me that you, or one of the others, betrayed her to Ketch. What do you know about it?'

Bowing stared at her, sullenly.

'She's a liar. She was always a nuisance, and we tried to help her. No one gave her away.'

'But Ketch knew where she had come from, and why,' insisted Dawlish.

'Well, I've told you there was a leakage at the H.O., haven't I?' said Bowing truculently. 'You'd better ask Clay, it's no use worrying me any more. I did all I could to help Yvonne, and the others, by enlisting your help, and see where that's got me!'

'You're a bit beside yourself,' said Dawlish quietly. 'We haven't time to wait until you've recovered either. It has to be worked out quickly. Yvonne, be quiet for a few minutes, and don't interrupt. Bowing, just what did she tell you?'

Bowing stared at the French girl, and then began to talk. His story coincided with hers down to the last detail, and Dawlish nodded with satisfaction, convinced that both were telling the truth, and that the mystery of Yvonne was solved. But there remained the reason why Ketch and the others had gone to such lengths in their attempt to kill her and Bowing. There remained the notes which she had transcribed, and the possibility that one or other of Bowing's party had played a double game.

He looked at a file which Trivett had sent from the Yard, and read the report on 'Yvonne Dubonnet', who was to be apprehended and extradited to Spain. That was further confirmation, and surely proof of the genuineness of the girl's story. The photograph was a poor one, and could have been of almost any girl.

Dawlish put it aside, and looked through the typewritten transcriptions of the conversation between Ketch and other men. There was nothing of particular interest, nothing to suggest why Ketch had been so anxious to take Yvonne away; no clue to the best course of action—except the possibility of an interview with Clay himself, and he did not think a great deal of the wisdom of a direct approach just then.

'I know what's the matter with *you*,' said Bowing in a tense voice. 'You're stuck, Dawlish, you don't know what to do next. You're nothing more nor less than a fraud.'

'You imbecile,' said Yvonne tensely, 'I no longer trust you, and nor does Captain Dawlish. But'—she turned her great eyes to Dawlish—'we *must* do something.'

Dawlish said: 'In good time we will.'

He sympathized to some degree with Bowing. There was so little prospect ahead of them, and the youngster had received a shock which would have affected many people to an even greater extent. For his part, Dawlish was confused with thoughts of Ketch, Clay and others, he could see nothing beyond them, while the fact that Whitehead had told him only half the truth created another difficulty. He was working in the dark, as it was intended that he should be. But, following the tragedy at the shed, this helplessness was disturbing.

'In good time,' sneered Bowing.

'Now look here,' began Ted Beresford, 'I—'

He stopped then, for the telephone rang.

It relieved the tension in the room, a tension caused as much by their impotence as Bowing's manner. It seemed as if each one of them expected the telephone to speak, to show an opening, to lead the way. As Dawlish leaned forward and picked it up, all eyes were upon him.

'Dawlish speaking,' he said.

'Whitehead here,' said Colonel Whitehead. 'I'd like you to come up to the office as quickly as you can, Dawlish. Can you manage that?'

The Colonel gave no indication of why Dawlish was wanted, but rang off immediately. In some ways it was an anti-climax, but to Dawlish there had been a note of urgency in his Chief's voice, an indication that more trouble was afoot.

Replacing the receiver, he said crisply:

'Whitehead wants me. You come, Ted, in case he meant us both. Look after the flat, Andy.'

He smiled briefly towards Felicity, put the transcribed notes and the extradition papers in his pocket and went downstairs with Ted. They walked in silence as far as Piccadilly, and there hailed a taxi.

On reaching Whitehall they were shown at once into Whitehead's office.

He nodded, grim-faced and unsmiling. 'How are you, Beresford? Now, Dawlish—what happened at Woking?'

Briefly, and to the point, Dawlish gave an account of the fire, a little concerned lest all that Whitehead wanted was just that.

At the end of the recital, Whitehead tapped his fingers on the desk thoughtfully.

'That doesn't seem to help much either way. Dawlish, you've had an idea that there's something much bigger behind this than you've so far known, haven't you?'

'I have,' said Dawlish, his heart beating a trifle faster.

'It's reached a stage where we've got to have action, and quickly,' said Whitehead. 'In the early hours of this morning a small internment camp at Drayton, kept for English Fascists and suspected Fifth Columnists, was partly destroyed by fire. Fifty-three of the internees escaped. Some have been recaptured, but a great number are at liberty.' He paused for a moment, as if to allow the full importance of what he had said to sink in, and then added quietly: 'The plan of the camp, kept at the Home Office, was stolen within the past three days. It's possible—mind you, I only say *possible*—that similar plans of other camps might also have been stolen. If that is so, it's beginning to look very much as if there is a carefully laid plot to release Fascists and Fifth Columnists. Somehow we have to stop it before it gets too large.'

CHAPTER FOURTEEN

WIDER SCOPE

When Dawlish and Beresford left Whitehall the newsboys were already yelling the news of the fire at Drayton Camp. There was little in the papers except a bare mention of the fire, and a generalization that the internees were being rounded up.

That there was much more behind it, Dawlish was now fully aware, although Whitehead had been able to give them little information.

He had given Dawlish a *carte blanche.*

For this Dawlish was profoundly grateful. Not only would it give him a wider scope, but it removed at once the feeling of frustration, the hopelessness of knowing that the motive for it all was deliberately being hidden from him. Whitehead had not revealed why he had created the impression that crucial knowledge was being kept up his sleeve, and in fact Dawlish imagined that he still kept some crumbs of it to himself. Its importance as far as Dawlish and the others were concerned seemed negligible. Now they had something to bite on.

They walked back to Audeley Street together, grimly happy in this knowledge.

To Dawlish the fact that Ketch was at large seemed the most important thing. More than he had realized turned on Ketch, and he cursed the fact that the man had escaped. But Whitehead had promised that the police would put out a general call for the man, who would then, if captured, be passed over to Dawlish for interrogation.

'*If* they get him,' said Beresford, gloomily.

'The trouble with this show is that we've started off on the wrong foot,' said Dawlish, with a certain amount of relish. 'We had a nasty blow when Neil went, and we haven't caught up on it yet. We're pulling up leeway all the time, but when we are level—' he paused for a moment, and as they turned towards the Admiralty Arch, his next words took Beresford completely by surprise.

'Don't look round and don't stop. We're being followed.'

Beresford said: 'Recognize anyone?'

'At long last, yes,' said Dawlish, conscious of a sharp rising of excitement. 'It's the chap who tripped Trivett up when Yvonne had her outing. He's got a long chin, I noted it at once for future reference. We'll stop at the Club. You go in, and I'll go on.'

A few minutes later Beresford strolled into the Carilon, but only as far as the foyer. When he saw the long-chinned man, he slipped out again, following the follower.

Dawlish slowed down a little; Beresford quickened his step. The distance between him and the long-chinned man decreased, until it was no more than a few yards. Then something seemed to warn the other; he stopped abruptly and half-turned.

He saw Beresford, who was smiling widely in anticipation, and darted into the road.

'Not this time, little one,' chanted Beresford. His arm shot out, clutching the flying coat.

The man turned and kicked at him viciously.

From the other side of the Mall a policeman came hurrying, and Dawlish, turning back, had his hand at his pocket to take out the card authorizing him to call on the police to help.

There was no warning, no indication that anything was wrong, but quite suddenly the long-chinned man gasped.

Beresford said: 'What the—'

The man had suddenly become a dead weight. He had to exert all his strength to prevent the fellow from falling. When he pulled him upright he saw the small red hole in his forehead, and he knew that the man had been shot; more, that he was dead.

'What is it?' snapped Dawlish.

Beresford lowered the body swiftly, and then moved across the road. Away towards St James's Park two men were hurrying. Dawlish left the startled policeman with the dead man, and joined in the pursuit.

The two men Beresford had seen now started to run.

Had the railings been about the park they would have had a more difficult task, but they jumped easily over the edging of stone-work in which the railings had been fixed. A dozen people were staring at them, and the policeman was blowing his whistle vigorously.

Dawlish reached Beresford.

They ran together and fell together, for neither of them saw the piece of twine stretched from one tree to another. In their haste they struck against it and pitched forward.

By the time they were on their feet again a little crowd had gathered about them, and the policeman had arrived with several of his fellows.

Dawlish felt too angry to say a word, and listened in silence to Beresford's exasperated summing up. 'My oath, but they mean business.'

'And *I* mean business,' said the constable grimly.

He was a large and ponderous-looking man, determined to have his say, but Dawlish's card, signed by the Assistant Commissioner of the Police and counter-signed by the Home Secretary, saw that it was a short one. The crowd was moved on as an ambulance arrived for the long-chinned man.

'Before he goes, I want to look through his pockets,' Dawlish said.

The policeman raised no objection, but the search was fruitless, yielding only a small collection of coppers. There were no keys in the man's possession, he had no wallet and no papers, and his handkerchief was without initials. He was a thin, pallid-faced fellow, and appeared to have died with no knowledge of what was coming to him.

'Ask Superintendent Trivett to see that his clothes are examined, will you?' Dawlish asked a sergeant who had taken over from the constable. 'I'll telephone him later.'

Dawlish and Beresford walked on, both a little bruised from the fall, but neither of them seriously hurt, except in their vanity. To Dawlish the fact that it had happened without him giving a thought to such an eventuality was the most mortifying thing; and it worried him, for he felt that he was losing his grip. There was justification for Bowing's earlier outburst, anyone of a hundred men could have done as much, or as little, as he had done.

In Piccadilly a newsboy was screeching:

'Fiff-columnists escape! Fiff-columnists escape!'

He was selling his papers fast, while Dawlish and Beresford passed him, tight-lipped, reaching the flat without speaking again. Tim Jeremy had returned, and appeared to be as depressed as the rest of them by the apparent *impasse*.

'Anything much?' Tim asked.

'It depends what you call much,' said Dawlish sourly. 'We know what it's about.' He told them a little, seeing Bowing's eyes widen, and hearing an exclamation from Yvonne. When he finished, keeping back only that which it was wiser for Bowing and Yvonne not to know, Felicity said quietly:

'So that's widened the scope.'

'What good is that when they haven't got a single idea between them!' sneered Bowing.

'You're wrong there.' said Beresford nastly. 'We've all got one very strong one.'

'Let him alone,' said Dawlish wearily. 'What about some beer?' He eyed Tim Jeremy, who brought bottles from the dining-room, and then added thoughtfully: 'The fire at the camp started just like the one at the woodshed. Some of these beggars have a supply of phosphorous-plus, we might find out if it's being made in England or was smuggled in. A point Whitehead can fix.' A little more cheerfully he telephoned the Colonel, who promised to do all that he could to obtain samples of the fire-raising material used both at the camp and at the Woking woodshed.

Dawlish's mind began working more swiftly, the indignity of his fall behind him.

The fires were being started by someone who had access to the camps—and to Woking. That was the one connection, the one thing which might eventually help them. Whoever had started the Woking fire was associated with the fire-raiser at the internment camp. Home Office officials visited those camps from time to time, and—

Dawlish leapt to his feet, and once again telephoned the Colonel.

'Can we find out who visited the Drayton Camp from the Home Office recently?'

'I'm finding out,' said Whitehead, 'and I'll send you word as soon as I can. I've just seen Trivett,' he added, 'and he's coming over to see you.'

'I'll wait for him,' Dawlish promised.

He replaced the receiver, and thoughtfully regarded the others. Bowing and Yvonne were problems: they were all ears for anything that was said, and now he had to cope with Bowing's hostility, he felt his tolerance at its lowest ebb. Had he been sure that neither Bowing nor Yvonne could lead to further developments it would have been simpler; but there remained the possibility that they had not been wholly frank, and they were also baits for Ketch. He knew of no bait which was likely to be stronger.

He rubbed his chin thoughtfully, contemplating them, and then went into the dining-room, beckoning Ted and Tim. When they closed the door on Bowing's angry exclamation, he said slowly:

'Bowing's a problem, and I want one of you to solve it. We can use Tony Grayling's flat, he left me a key. Will one of you take Bowing there, leaving Yvonne with Felicity, and stay around until we want him?'

'Tim's just right for that job,' said Beresford promptly.

'Oh no, not me,' said Tim Jeremy.

'One or other,' said Dawlish with a smile. 'The other staying here. Andy's coming with me when we decide on somewhere to go.'

'What I like about you is your generous spirit,' said Beresford darkly. 'Do you realize that all we've done so far is to play watchdog for you?'

Nevertheless, it was Ted who left, good-temperedly enough, for a flat in Brook Street, taking Bowing with him, a Bowing who glowered but did not openly protest. On her own with Felicity, Yvonne was likely to be much less of a problem. Dawlish thought a little girlish chatter on clothes and hairstyles would be just the thing to lessen the strain under which she had been living.

When Trivett arrived, Dawlish was looking through the transcribed notes. He handed them to Trivett.

'A conversation between Ketch and two other men, taken down by Yvonne Lejeune,' said Dawlish. 'I can't find anything in it, but your cypher-and-code Johnnies might. If they can't, try Whitehead.'

Trivett stowed them away in his pocket with a grunt of satisfaction. He had called at the Yard on his way from Whitehead's place, and received word of the shooting of the long-chinned man. He told them that there was nothing on the man's clothes to indicate where they had been bought, and:

'We might get some news if we circulate his description,' he added, 'but we won't be able to identify him any other way. We've got the call out for Ketch, but—' he shrugged his shoulders. 'We've got the woman Cromarty at Cannon Row, but she swears she doesn't know what business Cromarty was on, and when she was told that he was dead she laughed and said she ought to get some peace now.'

'A nice creature,' said Dawlish ironically. 'You've tried her about Ketch?'

'He used to call at the flat from time to time, but she was never allowed to hear what was said. You can have a shot at getting something from her, if you like.'

He stopped abruptly, at an exclamation from Dawlish.

'Now what's the matter?' he demanded.

'My dear Bill, it's come to me in a flash that we've been barking up the wrong tree. We have assumed that Yvonne and Bowing were the target for the woodshed holocaust—but *were* they? Or were the would-be murderers after Cromarty and Dibben in a bid to stop them talking? The same, of course, goes for the long-chinned man. If Bowing and Yvonne have been used as a blind, if Ketch pretended to be after them when he didn't really give a damn what happened to them, we've certainly been had for suckers.' Dawlish paused, then went on earnestly: 'Attention was turned towards Bowing and the others at the H.O., and now Ketch tries the same thing on me, to keep me watching and wondering about them, when there's someone else needing much more attention.'

'It could be,' conceded Trivett, 'but does that help, if you don't know who else is concerned?'

'Does it help!' exclaimed Dawlish. 'My dear Bill, it tells us nearly everything.'

He did not go further, and no one expected him to, least of all Trivett. He leapt to his feet, and without further preamble hustled Cunningham and Trivett out of the flat. A little breathlessly, Cunningham demanded:

'What's the hurry, Pat?'

'All in good time,' said Dawlish, 'it's no good putting the cart before the horse.'

'More especially if you're not even sure you've got a horse,' said Trivett disparagingly.

But Dawlish was not to be rattled. He waved good-humouredly to Trivett, who was about to return to the Yard, and began to walk smartly along the street, Cunningham lengthening his stride in an endeavour to keep up with him. Across Green Park he went, and then through to St James's, humming a little tune under his breath. Reaching a side-road leading to Victoria Street, he paused for the first time and said amiably:

'We're going to see Clay's flat.'

'I don't see why that pleases you so much,' said Cunningham.

'Every day Clay goes home to luncheon,' said Dawlish, 'according, that is, to Whitehead. He should be there now, and we'll have a little talk with him. We don't have to worry too much about arousing the gentleman's suspicions. The affair is urgent, and we've got to prevent anything else of a like nature brewing at the camps.'

'I still don't see—' began Cunningham.

'*Don't see?* Clay's brother died and left a house, didn't he?'

'Well?'

'Bowing and the others had the use of the cottage?'

'Supposing they did.'

'Supposing they did!' repeated Dawlish scornfully. 'Andy, wake up! Can't you see the direct line between Bowing and Company and Clay? It might not be with Bowing himself, it might be with Playfair, McFee or any of the poor beggars who were in the shed, but it was Clay who let them have the place, Clay who knew the position of the shed and its vulnerability. Bowing's always been sure that Clay was involved, and the cottage turn-out proves it pretty clearly. Ah, Burnham Mansions, Number 31,' he added, approaching a large block of flats with satisfaction.

'I'm rapidly coming to the conclusion that you're crazy,' said Cunningham resignedly.

'Have I ever denied it?' demanded Dawlish.

Entering the hall of Burnham Mansions, they were told by a porter that Sir Alfred Clay had gone upstairs three-quarters of an hour before, and as far as he, the porter, knew, had not come down again.

Following directions, Dawlish and Cunningham went up by the lift and found flat 31 easily enough. There was an atmosphere of luxury and comfort about Burnham Mansions, befitting so high an official's home. Even the bell which Dawlish pushed had a subdued note.

There was no answer.

Dawlish tried again, and then knocked, but there remained no answer. He frowned, eyeing the door thoughtfully. 'We couldn't break that down in a hurry, let's look at the back.'

They went towards a door marked 'emergency exit', found it unlocked and stepped on to an iron landing. It was easy to see the windows of Clay's flat from there, one of them being near enough to reach. Farther along they could see another set of emergency stairs.

Dawlish was leaning forward trying the window when he heard footsteps on the second iron staircase. Glancing across, he saw Ketch scurrying downward.

CHAPTER FIFTEEN

THIRD TIME UNLUCKY

'We won't lose him this time,' said Dawlish softly.

With his automatic in his hand, he waited until Ketch was half-way down the first flight, and then called clearly:

'Looking for me, Ketch?' Under his breath he murmured to Cunningham: 'Go down for him, Andy.'

Taken completely by surprise and only twenty yards away, Ketch stood transfixed on the iron staircase, staring at Dawlish and the gun. Then, as Cunningham reached the concrete court-yard below, an audible oath came from Ketch's lips and he started to run down the stairs, taking his chance of being shot.

'I don't think so,' murmured Dawlish.

He fired twice, aiming for the man's legs. He heard the sharp metallic sound as one bullet hit the staircase, and then saw Ketch stagger. Cunningham reached the man as he hit the concrete.

Without haste, Dawlish joined them.

'A slight leg wound,' said Cunningham, 'not as bad as he wants to make out.' He looked at Ketch without sympathy. 'What shall we do with him?'

'Take him back where he came from,' said Dawlish.

Ketch gasped: 'No, no, I can't go back there, I can't go back there!'

'You're going,' said Dawlish quietly.

'I can't, I tell you, I won't!' Wildly, uselessly, the man struck out at Dawlish, who evaded the blow easily enough. 'You mustn't go in there, you mustn't go in!'

Dawlish said: 'Why not?'

'I can't tell you, I—'

Then, to Cunningham's astonishment, Dawlish turned and raced up the stairs.

He reached the door through which Ketch had come, and found it unlocked. Just inside the passage was another door, with the number '31' on it, and the word: '*Tradesmen*'. The door was locked, but there were two glass panels. Dawlish crooked his arm and drove his elbow through one of them. The glass made a sharp explosive noise as it splintered, but Dawlish hardly waited for it to fall before inserting his hand and pushing back the inside lock.

He stepped into a kitchenette, and on to a foyer: five doors, all shut, opened from it. He turned the handle of one, looked inside, and saw a bedroom. The second was also a bedroom, but the third, a large room, was a combined dining-room and lounge.

The table was set for two, and a meal appeared to have been finished not long before.

Dawlish went out, and tried the fourth door.

As he opened it he saw a pair of legs stretched out on the carpet. He went in farther. A man's body was lying there, his head battered. He did not know whether the man was alive or dead, but had little doubt that it was Clay. With difficulty Dawlish dragged him out on to the landing, then rapped on the door of the next flat. He waited until he heard someone coming, and then returned to Clay's study. About him was an urgency and an almost desperate haste. He noticed that the drawers of a filing cabinet were open. Dawlish shuffled through the papers and threw them on the desk. One of a bunch of keys opened the desk drawers, and from these he took papers, books and oddments.

As he finished he heard footsteps in the passage, and an excited burst of talk. Then a shadow fell across the desk, and Cunningham said:

'What the devil are you doing, Pat?'

'This place is going to burn like the others,' said Dawlish sharply. 'Ketch has fixed it, and the more stuff we get out before it goes up the better chance we'll have. Are the police here yet?'

'A sergeant's just coming.'

'Tell him we want half-a-dozen men, and the fire squad,' said Dawlish. He did not look round, but gathering everything from the drawers he could carry, hurried with it into the passage. He was there when the policeman arrived, talking earnestly to Cunningham. Not unreasonably the policeman wanted to know why half-a-dozen men were needed.

Depositing the papers on the floor, Dawlish took out his wallet and handed the man his card, saying authoritatively: 'I want six men at least, to empty the flat, and the nearest fire brigade to stand by in readiness.'

'*Here*, sir?' The man looked round helplessly.

'Certainly here, and you can take my word for it that there's no time to lose.'

With Cunningham he began to lift the bookcases out of the room. Then he began to clear out the shelves. Once or twice he paused for a moment, to look at what appeared to be small, dark green cards, but he made no comment until Cunningham bent to retrieve one from the floor.

'Stop that, Andy!' his voice was urgent, and Cunningham drew his hand away quickly. 'That's the source of the trouble, I think,' he added. 'I hope the police have had the sense to warn the others nearby.'

'They're all roused,' said Cunningham confidently.

Back in the flat, Dawlish began to tap the walls. Eventually he found a small safe, opened by pressing a small boss in the picture rail. Cunningham stared in surprise.

'You do have ideas!'

'Get that stuff out,' said Dawlish shortly.

He was sweating a little, but surprised that he had had so long in which to work. For the first time doubt that Ketch had come to fire the place, after attacking Clay, reared up in his mind. Then he heard the clanging of the fire-bell, and through the windows saw an engine draw up outside.

'That sergeant's going to think harshly of you if nothing happens,' said Cunningham dryly.

'I'm going to think harshly of myself,' said Dawlish.

The policemen were taking the contents of the study down to the street, and the place was stripped of everything which might be of interest. Dawlish looked through the bedrooms, finding no papers, but discovering in the dining-room a briefcase with the monogram 'A.C.' He tucked it under his arm, while the sergeant, bewildered and a little affronted, stared about the wrecked study.

'I hope all this is necessary—' he began.

A sheet of flame from one of the fitted book-cases stopped his next words.

It shot outwards with a roar, and the room was suddenly filled with smoke and the smell of burning.

Someone started screaming.

Dawlish put a hand on Cunningham's arm, and dragged him

into the passage. The smoke was getting worse, and the flames were already at a white-heat. Firemen were running up ladders, while the flats next door to Clay's were being rapidly emptied of their occupants. Dawlish, less satisfied than vindicated, went downstairs with Cunningham by the back way.

'You left Ketch all right?' he asked shortly.

'With two policemen,' said Cunningham. 'I told them not to let him go, either in an ambulance or taxi—he was to stay there.'

'And where's there?'

'In the room of the caretaker's flat,' said Cunningham.

A small crowd had gathered in the courtyard, but allowed Dawlish and Cunningham to pass without hindrance. A uniformed policeman was standing by the door, and beyond him was a second man, standing over Ketch.

Dawlish ignored him, but spoke to the nearest constable.

'You've probably recognized this man as the "Ketch" or "Cartwright" you're looking for,' he said briefly. 'Telephone Scotland Yard, please, tell Mr Trivett that you have him and tell him that Captain Dawlish wants to remove him. Do that quickly, will you?'

'Yes, sir.' The man went towards a telephone and lifted the receiver, while Ketch turned blood-shot eyes towards Dawlish, and gasped:

'You've no right, you—'

'Shut up!' said Dawlish savagely.

'The—the police!' gasped Ketch. 'The law says—'

He stopped when the policeman began to talk into the telephone, and, after giving Dawlish's message, started a series of 'yes-sirs' and 'no-sirs'. He finished at last and turned, eyeing Dawlish with new respect.

'That's all right, sir, you can do as you wish.'

'Thanks,' said Dawlish. 'Get me a taxi, will you?'

'I ought to go to hospital,' shouted Ketch. 'I'm badly hurt, I need a doctor!'

Dawlish took no notice, but ran through the man's coat pockets. There was another wallet, replacing the one which Dawlish had taken the previous night. There was also a transparent envelope.

Inside were several of the small, dark green 'cards'.

'Well, well,' he said. 'All the evidence we need.'

Ketch drew a sharp breath but said nothing, and soon afterwards the taxi arrived. They walked through pools of water coming from the hoses now playing on the burning building. Regular firemen and A.F.S. men were busy, working the pumps and keeping the crowd back with the help of the police. The crowd gasped when Dawlish appeared, and it was obvious that Ketch, wrapped in a blanket and limping badly, was considered to be a victim. His pale face and wild eyes caused murmurs of sympathy as Dawlish helped him along, stony-faced, to the taxi, and climbed in with Cunningham after telling the driver to go to the Audeley Street flat.

Cunningham sat on a seat opposite Dawlish and the prisoner. Both were a little dishevelled, although Cunningham was far more presentable than he had been after the Brittling Hotel explosion and the fire at Woking. Neither of them spoke, and Ketch eyed first one and then the other, in agitated silence.

The cab drew up at last.

'Keep a look-out, Andy,' said Dawlish. 'We're probably being watched, they'll get Ketch if they have half a chance.'

There was no attempt to prevent them taking their prisoner up the stairs and into the flat, however. Dawlish took him into his bedroom, after Cunningham had told Felicity and the others something of what had happened. Felicity wanted to know whether any first-aid was needed, and for the first time since he had seen Ketch, Dawlish smiled.

'Bless your heart, no. Not yet, anyhow, and when we've finished with him he'll probably be past first-aid.'

'Oh!' ejaculated Yvonne.

'Don't waste your sympathy,' said Dawlish. He ran his hand through his crisp hair, and then said quietly: 'Tim, you'd better go to Burnham Mansions, Victoria Street, and look after the papers we took from Clay's flat—the police have them, but they'd better be looked through by us. Andy, will you find what hospital or mortuary they've taken Clay to, and go there if it's a hospital? One of us ought to be by his side in case he comes round.'

They left him almost immediately.

Dawlish went into the bedroom, locked the door, then turned and faced Ketch.

'L-listen to me, Dawlish—'

'Be quiet,' ordered Dawlish. 'This time you won't get away, I've one or two things to tell you. One is, that I'm an Intelligence Officer.'

Ketch's eyes widened; surprise and dismay filled them.

'As such I can treat you as I want,' said Dawlish; 'I am responsible to no one but my own superiors. I work on my own responsibility when it looks necessary, and I do exactly what I think I should. If it means a beating-up, I beat up. If it means going a stage further, I go that stage.' He was speaking slowly and deliberately, calculating the effect of his words on the other man. He was exaggerating, of course, as he meant to exaggerate.

He went on:

'I've been given instructions to find who is starting these fires, who freed the internees from Drayton Camp and who is giving you help from the Home Office. Before I've finished with you I'm going to have the answer to all three questions.'

Ketch gasped:

'I—I'm not the Boss, I only take orders—'

'Dibben told me exactly the same, yet to make sure he didn't tell me too much, you had him killed. You burned eight people alive to do that, Ketch. You blew up the Brittling Hotel, and killed several people, you arranged for your long-chinned friend to be shot while Beresford and I were closing in on him. You attacked Clay, and you left the fire-cards at his flat, with the intention of burning the place down. You did all of that, Ketch, but now you've come to the end of the road. I'm going to turn you inside out, and if I have to smash you bone by bone I'll make a job of it.'

Ketch gasped: 'I had to do it! I had orders. If I hadn't—'

'If you're going to tell me that your miserable life would have been taken if you'd refused, don't ask for sympathy,' said Dawlish. 'Listen to me, Ketch. Of all the things you've done, the worst is to help the enemies of this country. That, in wartime, is the ultimate crime.' He removed his coat, and then rolled up his sleeves. Brows knitted, he stepped to the dressing-table where there were two candles in a silver sconce. He lit one of them, calculating each action to strike terror into Ketch's heart. Holding it high, he added: 'Fire hurts more than most things, Ketch, and you'll be able to guess what those poor beggars at Woking felt like.'

As he stepped forward, Ketch began to scream.

CHAPTER SIXTEEN

THE EFFECTS OF SIR ALFRED CLAY

Dawlish opened the door and faced the two girls.

'Has he talked?' asked Felicity quickly.

'Certainly he talked,' said Dawlish, 'and I can assure you, without being touched.' Felicity heaved a sigh of relief, and he looked at her quizzically. 'If he hasn't lied—and I don't think he was in a mood for lying—all of the half-dozen chaps of the Dibben and Cromarty fraternity get their orders direct from him. No Ketch, no orders for the roughnecks, and certainly there'll be no Ketch for a long time to come. We're getting on.'

'Is—is that all?' asked Yvonne unsteadily.

'Not by a long way,' Dawlish assured her. 'Ketch has been in contact with Sir Alfred Clay, who was one of the bad-hats at the Home Office. Ketch thinks there are others, but he only knows of Clay. And this morning he had instructions to get rid of him.'

'From whom?' Felicity demanded quickly.

'There's the rub,' admitted Dawlish. 'Ketch says he doesn't know, and again I believe him. He had a letter giving him the order this morning, and he burned it after he'd read it, a routine procedure, it seems. He's never made personal contact with them, but always acted on written or telephoned orders. He doesn't know whether they're Government officials, or Nazis in England. All he knows is that they've paid him a lot of money for his filthy work.'

'Can't we trace anything through that?' Felicity wanted to know.

'Payment in hard cash,' said Dawlish, 'always in one-pound notes which aren't easy to trace.' He shrugged. 'Ketch admits blowing up the Brittling Hotel, but swears that he doesn't know why he had the orders. Then he received some of the fire-cards, and was told to prevent anyone relaying information to me or others. So he went after everyone at the Cottage, because one—just one,' added Dawlish, and looked intently at Yvonne, 'of Bowing's friends knows more than he should.'

'And that one was?' asked Yvonne sharply.

'He says that he doesn't know,' Dawlish told her, 'and that might also be true. But to proceed: when we caught Cromarty and Dibben he decided to liquidate them before they gave anything away. He chose the time and place to give us the idea he was after Bowing and his friends. He also planned the murder of the long-chinned man. His killer can be found at the Koestler Hotel, Paddington, with the rest of his roughnecks. Then orders came through to put Clay out and burn up the flat.'

Felicity said rather coldly: 'You aren't really very much further on, are you?'

'Great Scott, what more do you want out of one little crook?' demanded Dawlish in an injured voice. 'He confirms, or explains, pretty well everything we need up to Clay, and he admits the tie-up between himself, Clay and the Drayton Camp business. He went to lunch with Clay, before attempting to kill him. But Ketch made it plain enough that Clay was the receiver, not the giver, of orders.'

'That's what I mean,' said Felicity.

'Yet he must have known something dangerous to the plotters,' Dawlish said, 'otherwise, why kill him? The most important thing to me so far,' he continued, 'is to know that it was Ketch who was the operations manager of the outfit. Now that he's out of action we haven't so many people to deal with, and we ought to be able to walk about with reasonable security.' He chuckled. 'That's a relief, Yvonne, isn't it?'

'If it is true,' said Yvonne.

'Oh, the odds against us are reduced all right,' Dawlish assured her.

He judged from Felicity's expression that she believed he was holding something back, but in fact he had told her the gist of what Ketch had admitted.

He telephoned Whitehead with a brief report, and arranged with Trivett that the residents at the Koestler Hotel, near Paddington Station, be watched. Then came a call from Tim, to say that all of Clay's papers were safe and that he had put them in a taxi: should he take them to the Yard, or to the flat?

'Bring 'em here, we'll have a session on records,' said Dawlish. 'How long will you be?'

'About twenty minutes.'

'I'll be here,' Dawlish promised him.

Hardly had he replaced the receiver than Andy Cunningham called, to say that Sir Alfred Clay had died a few minutes after being admitted to hospital, without recovering consciousness. His young son, a sub-lieutenant on leave, was now at the hospital demanding to be told more of what had happened.

Dawlish said thoughtfully: 'What have the police said to him?'

'Next-to-nothing. But someone mentioned your name, and it wouldn't surprise me if he doesn't turn up, breathing vengeance. I thought you'd better know. Is there anything else I can do here?'

'No-o,' said Dawlish, 'but you can telephone the Woking hospital, and find out how McFee and the others are. If there's any chance of them being released, keep your eyes on them.'

'That's a bit vague, isn't it?' demanded Cunningham.

'As positive as I can make it,' Dawlish told him. 'Give me a ring as soon as you've heard from the hospital.'

As Dawlish replaced the receiver there was a sharp ring at the front door.

'That might be young Clay,' said Dawlish.

When he opened the door a fresh-faced man of perhaps twenty-five years stood on the threshold. The caller was dressed in the uniform of a sub-lieutenant. He had a square, aggressive chin thrust well forward, and at the moment his eyes were narrowed and hard.

'Captain Dawlish?' he asked abruptly. 'My name is Clay, Adam Clay.'

'I was hoping you'd come,' said Dawlish. He turned and led the young man into the flat, introducing him to Felicity and Yvonne.

Adam Clay's pleasant voice was a little taut, and he gave the impression that he was suffering from a considerable emotional strain. Obviously he was ill-at-ease with Yvonne and Felicity, and Dawlish led the way into the dining-room, indicating an easy-chair.

'Now exactly why did you come?' he asked.

'Why did you expect me?' retorted Clay.

'Because I'd been told that you were at the hospital and that I was mentioned,' said Dawlish quietly.

'I see.' Clay's words were clipped. 'Look here, Dawlish, you understand what happened, don't you? I've just got home on leave. I found the flat gutted, and heard someone saying that my father had been murdered. I found that was true. I asked the police for information, and they were extremely vague. I'm not going to be put off with vagueness. I'm home for a month, and by God I'll find out who killed my father before I go back.'

Dawlish said: 'I've got the man.'

Clay started forward in his chair.

'You've *caught* him? You mean he's under arrest?'

'Very much so,' Dawlish said, not liking the prospect before him, but knowing that it was unavoidable. 'The trouble is, Clay, that you're going to get a nasty shock and hear things that you won't like. The police weren't keen on telling you, but—'

'Do you mind telling me *exactly* what you mean?' demanded Clay stiffly.

Dawlish picked up an evening paper, folded it to the Drayton Camp story and handed it to Clay. He read it quickly, then looked up, bewildered.

'This has nothing to do with me.'

'There's reasonable evidence that your father had something to do with it,' said Dawlish quietly.

Clay snapped: 'Are you mad?'

'Look here,' said Dawlish. 'The papers from your father's flat are coming here soon, and I'm going through them. I have the necessary authority,' he added quietly, 'and I don't see why you shouldn't lend a hand. You can take out anything of a private nature, and it will convince you that we're quite serious in suspecting that your father wasn't all that he seemed.'

Clay's hands clenched.

'I've never heard such madness in my life,' he said tersely. 'It's utter tripe. Father wouldn't—'

Dawlish interrupted him:

'All the evidence points the other way, I'm afraid.'

'What evidence? And what the devil has it got to do with you? What are you trying to get *me* to do?'

'Help to clear this business up,' said Dawlish quietly. 'I don't yet know how you can, but I fancy you'd rather be at hand in case an opportunity arises.' He felt ill-at-ease, imagining the blow that the news was for the youngster. 'As for the evidence—'

He went on to tell Adam Clay of the many things that had happened, omitting only those which did not directly concern his father. The young man sat with drawn face and tightly clenched fists until the narrative was finished, then walked abruptly towards the window. He did not turn when Tim Jeremy rang the front door bell—Tim had a pile of papers and books in his arms, and a taxi-driver, also loaded, stood behind him.

'Come and give us a hand, Clay, will you?' Dawlish called.

Adam Clay, moving very stiffly, Felicity, Yvonne and the others, went downstairs to empty the taxi between them.

Then began a scrutiny of them, Dawlish selecting one pile, running through the papers, passing on to Adam Clay anything clearly personal. Dawlish found a deed of adoption, but made no comment; it proved that Adam Clay was not the knight's natural son. They worked for over two hours before the girls went to make tea, and at half-past six they were still busy.

Nothing of exceptional interest was discovered until Yvonne gave a sharp exclamation.

'What's there?' asked Dawlish, seeing a sheaf of papers in her hand. He stretched out for them.

'It is so hard to believe,' said Yvonne, relinquishing the papers with some reluctance. 'You see—the play.'

'Play?' interjected Adam Clay.

Dawlish looked down at the MS. of a play, seeing the names of the characters in red on the left-hand side, the text of the dialogue in black opposite it. He glanced at one or two lines, but they were ordinary enough, somewhat prosy, and bringing Playfair to mind at once.

'Why should he have a copy of it?' demanded Yvonne.

'He was always interested in amateur dramatics,' said Adam Clay quietly. 'He—what's the matter, Dawlish?'

The sailor broke off as Dawlish suddenly stopped turning over the folios, staring grim-eyed at one of them. The folio was headed: '*Characters in order of their Appearance*.'

The name of the first character was Monckton *Drayton*.

'The first character, the first internees' camp to be opened up,' said Dawlish breathlessly. He leapt up, hurrying into the other room for the telephone. 'If the other characters have internment camp names, we've struck something big at last.'

CHAPTER SEVENTEEN

NAMES MAKE NEWS

'Hallo,' said Superintendent Trivett, 'what's the trouble now?' He paused while Dawlish asked him whether he knew, off-hand, the names of internment camps throughout the country. 'Most of them, yes.'

'Is there one called Mattley?'

'In Somerset, yes,' said Trivett.

With studied calm Dawlish read the third character's name. 'Tanton?'

'In Yorkshire.'

'Borlash?'

'In Argyllshire, I think. Somewhere in Scotland, anyhow.'

'That's good enough,' said Dawlish. 'Bill, we've found the camps likely to be affected. Will you telephone the Woking police, and tell them to follow McFee, Playfair and the girl Larkin, if they should leave hospital? Andy Cunningham will probably be on the way down there, but he'll need help. If you've time to send some of your brightest men down it would be safer. Will you arrange it, one way or the other?'

'Yes,' said Trivett, 'but what's it about?'

'The play is the code,' said Dawlish quietly. 'It's not a gentle relaxation for frightened minds, as we thought. Mattley's next on the list, and the quicker they're warned that something might be breaking down there the better.' He paused a moment, and then added urgently: 'Tell them to look out for some little green cards. They're to be careful how they're picked up—they mustn't be touched with the bare hand. This is most important. Will you fix that too?'

Trivett drew a deep breath.

'Right. I'll come over immediately afterwards.'

'That's fine,' said Dawlish. 'Oh, and who visited Drayton from the Home Office recently?'

'I was going to tell you that,' said Trivett. 'Clay did, with several others.'

'Who were the others?'

'Sir Mortimer Fraser, and some lesser officials.'

'Bowing's immediate chief,' said Dawlish thoughtfully. 'It doesn't seem as if we have to look further than Clay for that, but we can't be sure. Who's been to Mattley Camp lately?'

'I don't know, but I'll find out and tell you when I come over.'

Dawlish replaced the receiver, deep in thought.

Then he put his hand to his inside breast-pocket and drew out an envelope. From this he took the record of the conversation between Ketch and the others, and glanced through it quickly. No one moved until he spoke.

'Well, well, so we're on to something big at last. Drayton's mentioned here—Ketch was going to "see him" yesterday. And he was going to see "Mattley" today. My oath, I hope they're in time!' He stood quite still, rubbing his chin, before saying: 'Tim, go over to Grayling's flat, and bring Ted here. Have young Bowing taken to Cannon Row, it won't do him any harm to cool his heels there for a bit, and it will free Ted. I wish Andy would report,' he added a little peevishly. 'He should have been through long ago.'

He could not know that Andy Cunningham was in a London hospital, unconscious, with nothing in his pockets to identify him, suffering from some kind of poisoning which was creating something of a problem for the doctors. Trivett had no word of it when he came, bringing with him the news that Sir Mortimer Fraser and Sir Alfred Clay, with their entourage, had visited the Mattley Internment Camp, in Somerset, two days before. Mattley had been telephoned to look for the phosphorous-plus cards, and for an outbreak of trouble.

It was quite dark by then.

The black-out curtains were drawn, and Trivett and Dawlish were alone in the dining-room when the telephone rang sharply.

Dawlish left Trivett, picked up the telephone and heard Tim Jeremy's voice, set on a grim note. He stiffened at the sound of it, preparing for bad news. It came quickly.

'Ted's been knocked out, he isn't too good. Bowing's gone, without a trace.'

Dawlish stared at the instrument, before saying sharply:

'Where's Ted now?'

'It's a hospital job.'

'So we haven't caught the roughnecks yet,' said Dawlish, 'I thought we had them. Look after Ted, and come here as soon as you can.'

He replaced the receiver, but had not passed on the news before the telephone rang again; this time it was Scotland Yard with a message for Trivett. The Superintendent came to the 'phone at once. Watching him Dawlish saw his hand tightening about the instrument, his expression sobering.

'All of them?' he said after a pause, and then: 'Right. Have a general call put out . . . you have? . . . good.' He put down the receiver, and turned to Dawlish. 'McFee, Playfair and the girl were removed from Woking Hospital at dusk, in a fake ambulance supposed to have been sent from the Yard. There's a general call out for it.'

'How inadequate can one feel?' Dawlish asked hopelessly. 'There isn't anything we've managed to do right, yet, except the interview with Jack Ketch.'

'What are we going to do *now*?' demanded Yvonne finally.

Dawlish shook his head as if at a distracting bee, and turned to Trivett. 'For the time being, Bill, I think Mattley's a good idea, don't you? Tim had better come with us. Clay, do you want a trip?'

'Yes,' said Adam Clay promptly.

'Good man. Bill, will you have three or four of your hearties brought here at once, in case there's any attempt to cause trouble at the flat? You'll stay right here, Fel, won't you—no venturing out for either you or Yvonne until the worst of this is over.'

'But why go to Mattley?' demanded Felicity.

'They must have a contact-man inside,' said Dawlish, 'and we may just be in time to stop a wholesale escape. We'd better go by 'plane,' he added, and immediately telephoned Whitehead, reporting as much as was necessary and receiving his chief's assurance that a cabin-'plane would be waiting for the party at Heston as soon as he reached there. In exactly fifteen minutes Tim had returned, and with Trivett, Dawlish and Clay, left Audeley Street in Trivett's car, for the aerodrome. They boarded a two-engined machine just before eight o'clock and expected to be at the landing ground near Mattley Internment Camp soon after nine. They were half-way there when the fires started at Mattley.

The internees at Mattley were mostly Italian. They were kept in a wire-enclosed encampment, spreading over some twenty acres. Most of them were housed in army huts, while those in poor health, or those who had earned special privileges, were held in a large house within the encampment.

Colonel James Maitland, the O.C., had been badly shaken by the news of the fire and the escapes at Drayton. He had doubled his guards, and once word had been sent through he had arranged for a search of the camp and the grounds, for the little green cards.

He found none, although it was obvious to the guards that the prisoners were restive and on edge. That might have been because of the more stringent precautions during the day, but Maitland was afraid that it was because they knew that something was brewing. Two mild encounters between guards and the more insolent prisoners were reported before dusk, but that was not exceptional: the younger men were always giving trouble.

At half-past eight, Maitland started a round of visits himself. From one of the huts came the sound of music, and raucous voices raised in song. From another he heard the click of billiard balls as games were in progress. In the reading-room, thirty or forty prisoners were bent over books they had borrowed from the extensive library.

Everything seemed normal.

Outside it was very dark. A cold wind blew from the east, bringing a fine, driving rain. It whistled through the trees beyond, making Maitland peer about him as he moved from hut to hut.

That finished, he inspected the guards. Normally one man patrolled every fifty yards of the wire stockade: that night he had two for every thirty yards.

At every post he had the same assurance:

'All quiet, sir.'

In the opinion of the sergeant who accompanied the Colonel, the old boy had the wind-up without cause; nothing would happen at Mattley, and the fellows at Drayton had been too damned careless. Thinking thus, the sergeant stifled a yawn, while Maitland looked at his illuminated wrist-watch.

'Just turned half-past eight,' he muttered. 'We'll have a look at the searchlights, sergeant.'

They turned from a gate guarded by four men, and went towards the searchlight battery, the prime duty of which—though called into operation against enemy aircraft when the need arose—was to light up the camp should an escape-attempt be made.

Through the howling wind the faint sounds of music could be heard from one of the huts. Yet Maitland was not reassured.

Battling onward, they were some twenty yards from the battery when a flash of flame shot fifty feet into the air. Maitland and the sergeant flung themselves flat on their faces, waiting for an explosion which did not come.

Instead, a sharp hissing sound could be heard, and as they leapt to their feet they saw the battery dissolve in a mass of flames. Maitland rushed towards the huts, while the wailing of the 'escape' siren added to the whine of the wind, eerie and high-pitched.

Another burst of flame came from one of the gates, and fast upon it a rattle of shooting, *from outside.* Maitland saw a man, silhouetted against the flames, fall suddenly as he levelled his rifle. Others fell, and then a dozen or more men rushed towards the wire, cutting it swiftly and expertly although under fire from the guards who had rushed to the spot.

The fires were increasing, springing up in every corner of the camp, as, not one man, not twenty, but two hundred or more ran from the huts towards the gap in the wire. They ignored the shooting, but then the shooting was nothing to worry about, for the flames were springing up even from the ground; no guard could be sure that he would not be engulfed suddenly in a fierce heat. Confusion reigned everywhere.

Maitland, hard-faced, stood his ground and watched, realizing his own helplessness. He waited for five minutes, then made his way to his office. He had given instructions for word to be sent at the least sign of trouble. By then, too, the fire squad was on duty, and the Commands of all regiments within a fifty miles radius were being informed on the telephone and by radio. Maitland peered bleakly about him, while the sergeant who had remained with him throughout the disturbance, white-faced and remorseful, avoided his stare. Both knew that nothing more could be done; the whole countryside had been alerted, but the camp itself was a mass of flames.

It was visible to Dawlish and his party as their 'plane drew within sight of Mattley.

With orders to land, the pilot called instructions to the machine-gunners in the front and rear turrets, and then put the nose of the machine towards the aerodrome nearby. By then machine-gun fire was visible near the aerodrome, where the Defence Corps was in action.

The 'plane landed without difficulty, and was approached immediately by a small squad. Dawlish and the others climbed out near the control-tower, seeing the fire about two miles away, increasing in intensity. Beyond the barbed wire which surrounded the landing field men could be seen running in all directions.

'It looks as if you're too late,' Adam Clay said.

'It seems to be a habit of mine,' said Dawlish stiffly. In the yellowish light his face looked gaunt and sombre. 'You know, Bill,' he added to Trivett, 'this is only half the show. They get away, but unless they've someone conveniently handy to hide them, most of them are bound to be rounded up. If we can't stop the ruddy break-outs, we can at least find out where they're going.'

'That's the question,' said Trivett bleakly. 'Can we?'

CHAPTER EIGHTEEN

WHERE DO THEY GO?

Colonel Whitehead, called to a special conference at Downing Street that night, asked the same question. Number 10 had, of course, been kept advised of what was happening, but the second outbreak in twenty-four hours demanded special attention and prompt action. Whitehead, who knew that Dawlish was held in considerable regard by several of the men seated around the table in the big room, wondered what they would say now.

'Yes,' he said, when the Under-Secretary to the Home Office asked whether Dawlish had been working on the case without hindrance, 'but only for the past few days.' He gave a brief summary of what had happened, including the part which Captain Parmitter had played, and then added: 'Dawlish has my complete trust, of course.'

The Under-Secretary said:

'Yes, yes, we know that, but he isn't showing very promising results this time. We can't afford to fail again and again.'

'No one is more aware of it than Dawlish,' said Whitehead strongly, 'and to be fair, we must acknowledge that he hasn't had a square deal on this business, you know. We haven't confided in him, or at least we didn't until the last minute, when the plans were made. He has caught the man Ketch, he discovered the order in which the attempts are to be made—'

'Attempts!' exclaimed the Under-Secretary witheringly. 'I'd call them full-scale operations.'

The Deputy Prime Minister, at the head of the table, was a mild-mannered man with a well-developed faculty for listening, which, nevertheless had its limits. He looked with resignation from one man to the other, and then said briefly:

'The source of the trouble appears to be in your Department, Kay.' The Under-Secretary coloured a little, hesitated and then said sharply:

'It was known that there was something disturbing happening, but Whitehead kept too much of it to himself.'

'Justifiably, I think,' said the Deputy P.M. 'But we haven't time to worry about that. Our job is to stop further repetitions. The order of outbreaks can be altered, of course. Unless we can see some way of insuring against further trouble, and I don't think we can, we will have to move the internees. There is nothing else to be done.'

'There's nowhere for them to go,' the Under-Secretary protested.

'We must find somewhere,' said the Deputy P.M.

'And Dawlish?' asked Whitehead bluntly.

'He had best carry on,' said the Deputy P.M. He looked about the table for confirmation, and if there were those who doubted the wisdom of his decision, only the Under-Secretary voiced them. He was dissatisfied with Dawlish's handling of the case, he said, and for that matter with Whitehead's department. He made it clear that he felt affronted because he had not been told of the suspicions earlier. Much of the trouble could have been avoided, he suggested, had the matter not been kept so secret.

The Deputy P.M. smiled.

'Yes, Kay, we can understand that, but Whitehead had his instructions from here. The immediate problem is—how long will it take us to move the prisoners from the camps?'

'Is there anything more you need me for?' asked Whitehead. 'Dawlish is due back with a report in an hour's time.'

'I don't think so, thank you,' said the Deputy P.M., mildly.

Whitehead, disturbed and disgruntled as well as troubled, left Number 10 and walked across to his office, where the night staff was waiting, keyed up because of the news from Mattley. There was a message from Dawlish, who had reached Heston at five o'clock—it was then five-thirty; he could be expected at any minute.

'H'm, yes,' said Whitehead. 'I'll see him in my office.'

Looking tired, but very much himself, Dawlish greeted the night staff, then went into Whitehead's room. Whitehead indicated an easy-chair, and pushed over cigarettes.

'So it's going against us, Dawlish.'

'Where do they go,' said Dawlish. 'That's what we have to worry about. The O.C. at Mattley estimates that at least seventy men and a dozen women have escaped. They can't just disappear into thin air.'

'Think you can handle it?' asked Whitehead abruptly.

'I haven't the faintest idea,' said Dawlish. 'It's gone beyond our usual sphere now, of course.' He did not say what was in his mind, that if he had been in the affair from the start he would have had a much better chance. 'Have you seen higher authority yet?'

'You're still on the job,' said Whitehead.

'I suppose I ought to be thankful for that,' said Dawlish gloomily. 'But damn it, we're stuck all night. Bowing, McFee, Playfair and the girl have gone. Over a hundred internees too, probably to the same place, and I haven't the faintest idea where it is. I'm just running round in circles.'

'Steady,' said Whitehead quietly.

'Sorry, sir,' said Dawlish with a tired smile, 'but I've never struck anything quite like this in my life.' He stubbed out his cigarette, and eyed his Chief frankly. 'I can't make a single suggestion, that's the truth of it.'

'Nothing at all, eh?' said Whitehead raising his eyebrows. 'That's very unlike you. Almost unprecedented I should say.'

'But there it is,' said Dawlish. 'I've a feeling that this affair is even bigger than we realize, that we're being deliberately blinded. It was mild enough when it started. Then it gradually widened, until Clay got in it, and the Bowing clique got kicked out; and now the general escape. What else is going to happen?'

'Isn't this bad enough?' said Whitehead.

'That won't stop it from getting worse,' said Dawlish sharply. '*Why* do they want these people free? What's behind it? What big difference does it make? All of them are well known, there'll be a look-out for them everywhere, they haven't much chance of getting into factories and doing odd spots of sabotage. There might be a few isolated cases of that, but an occasional escape would be the best way of handling it. Why a hundred or more of them? And why plan to release thousands?'

Whitehead said quietly:

'Just what are you thinking?'

'I can't see through it,' said Dawlish, 'but I'm damned sure there is something else. What are they going to do? Arm the beggars, and let 'em loose as a kind of guerrilla band? It sounds fantastic, but can you think up a better idea?'

'No-o,' admitted Whitehead, frowning. 'I don't even like thinking of that one. It would mean supplies of arms and ammunition, a carefully co-ordinated organization.'

'The organization is there all right,' said Dawlish. 'We don't have to look far for that. They can get the phosphorous-plus into the camps without any trouble, no easy task.' He stopped, then frowned, his view suddenly sharpening. 'No *easy* task! Damn it, nothing's easier. They could pack the leaflets inside the air-proof containers and send them by post.'

'Come,' said Whitehead. 'There is a censorship.'

'Parcels and letters are opened, yes,' said Dawlish, 'but the containers could be inside the wrapping. What happens to the wrapping at the camps? Usually parcels are opened, the contents examined and then roughly re-fastened. Cakes, slab-chocolate—I needn't enumerate. And these things could be in any of them. A scrutiny of the parcels to Tanton tomorrow is called for, I think, sir. News of what is brewing could easily be sent in code, there might even be a series of plays. Most prison camps have their own society, and the plays are sent from outside. No one would stop a number of books containing plays from going in, and the things could be privately printed. It might even be Playfair's own effort.'

'When did you think this up?' Whitehead asked, already stretching for the telephone.

'I didn't. It's just come,' said Dawlish. 'Now we've two lines to take, sir, the post to the camps, and the hiding-place of the escapees. The first might lead to the second.' He pushed his chair back as Whitehead spoke into the telephone, and stood staring at his Chief while the latter talked on the long distance line to the O.C. at Tanton Camp. He was a long time talking, but he arranged the necessary inspection of wrappings from parcels, and for the next morning's post to be stopped before going to the prisoners.

Whitehead finished speaking, and replaced the receiver.

'He's worried, of course. They all are. Well, now the next thing is that most of the prisoners will probably be removed from the various camps during the day. It's a wise precaution, I think.'

Dawlish said sharply: 'What's that?'

Patiently Whitehead told him what was being arranged.

'Move them away from the camps?' repeated Dawlish blankly. 'But that's just damned silly. If these cards go to the prisoners by post, they'll get to them anyhow. And'—he drew a deep breath—'I'm just beginning to see the full possibilities, sir. These inflammable cards. Imagine a few of them in the G.P.O. Or at Scotland Yard, any of the Government Departments. You've never seen them go off, if you had—' he stopped abruptly, then added: 'Have you discovered anything about the source of supply?'

'No,' said Whitehead. 'The samples you took from Ketch have been examined, and they're not known in this country. Dawlish, what the devil are you talking about?'

'Those leaflets being sent up and down the country, and starting fires everywhere,' said Dawlish impatiently. 'There isn't a better way of destroying records, and while we're chasing round after escaped internees and a few people we think are in the show, they can be doing enormous harm.' He pointed towards a steel filing-cabinet in Whitehead's office, and snapped: 'Supposing there was one in that? All those records would be burned out before we could do a thing to stop it!'

Whitehead said: 'There isn't the slightest evidence to prove that you're right.'

'Do we have to wait for evidence?' demanded Dawlish, 'in other words, for disaster to strike again? My oath, what a bluff! All eyes concentrated on the Home Office and the internees, the least important thing of the whole show. Bowing given to us, to lead us to Clay. Clay killed, to keep us hunting his murderer. Ketch knowing little or nothing, and—oh, but what's the use of talking! There's only one imperative thing to be done. *Find the source of those inflammable cards.* We haven't any real evidence of any particular individual being concerned, we can't be sure that Bowing and the rest aren't baits to draw us in the wrong direction, a cool and calculated diversion, to keep us away from the main assault. I know it might not be,' he added and there was a harder note in his voice, 'and that for all you know I'm gibbering, but I've been scared of this thing since it started, it just didn't lead anywhere. But now I think I see.'

Whitehead spoke after a long pause.

'You may be right, Dawlish, but you're a bit muddle-headed, you know. How can it affect the main issue if the internees are moved from one place to another?'

Dawlish said: 'There was outside help, wasn't there?'

'Yes, but not strong, I gather.'

'Have we any chance of getting at the leaders without taking prisoners from the outside agents?' demanded Dawlish. 'If we move the internees there's no chance of another attack, and we'll have no guide at all. I can't say too emphatically that the internees ought to be left where they are, sir, with strong protecting forces surrounding the camps. Can you arrange that, d'you think?'

'I can suggest it,' said Whitehead. He eyed Dawlish steadily, still slow-speaking and urbane, although obviously more moved than he liked to show. 'You get to your flat and have some sleep, Dawlish. There's no point in you cracking up for want of rest. If anything develops that you should know, I'll have you called, and I'll do all I can to get the arrangements for transferring the internees postponed.'

Dawlish was silent for a moment, and then said:

'Right. Forty winks won't come amiss, either!'

Whitehead put a hand on his shoulder. 'I know what you're feeling, Dawlish. You haven't had the breaks, and you've been neither one thing nor the other. You aren't a freelance, and you aren't a policeman. You have to try to keep everybody happy, and'—Whitehead shrugged—'that's not so easy. But you don't need telling that you have my backing.'

'I know,' said Dawlish, and smiled briefly.

He went by taxi to Audeley Street, his mind confused with the ideas which had crowded into it while he had talked to Whitehead. That was his trouble; ideas did not come from patient thinking, they took hold of him and shook him in sudden bursts.

Through the mists of the affair he had seen the possibility that the Home Office angle was not the main one, that attention had been drawn towards it with a cunning which did not make it look too obvious. If he were right and something much bigger was pending, how could it be stopped?'

Felicity was up when he arrived.

Tim had returned to the flat instead of going with Dawlish, and Adam Clay had gone to his club, promising to look in the next day. He had been oddly silent on the way back, as if realizing the full implications of the business and trying to face the fact that his father was deeply implicated.

Felicity, obviously, had been troubled until Tim's return, but she was smiling when Dawlish arrived, and cheerful enough. She suggested tea, but Dawlish said that all he wanted was sleep. She looked at his grey face with quick, sympathetic eyes, and hustled him into the bedroom. Then, with a stern admonition to everyone in general not to make a noise, crept out and closed the door.

Adam Clay called at the Audeley Street flat at half-past twelve, and was admitted by Yvonne. If she saw the way his eyes lighted up at sight of her, she made no sign.

'How is Dawlish?' he asked, obviously for something to say.

'He's just having a bath,' said Yvonne.

'A shattering event,' he said dryly.

'Nothing else happened?'

'Not yet,' Yvonne told him, 'although the telephone has been ringing all the morning. I've taken notes of the messages for Captain Dawlish.'

Before he listened to the notes, which Yvonne had taken down in shorthand at the telephone, however, Dawlish spent a few minutes talking with Clay. His earlier impression that the youngster was both sensible and level-headed was strengthened as Clay opened the conversation without any preamble.

'I've faced up to it, Dawlish, and I've seen the policeman, Trivett. There's just nothing to say or do, except that I want to help all I can.'

'Good man,' said Dawlish. 'We can use you.'

Tim Jeremy came in then, saying how hungry he was.

It lightened the atmosphere, and they all laughed as Felicity and Yvonne rushed to cupboards and pantry to see what could be found in the way of food. A meal of sorts, satisfying but a little sketchy, was soon in full swing.

As Tim and Dawlish continued to eat heartily, Yvonne settled back in her chair and started to read out her notes of the tele-phone conversations.

'At 9.15,' she read, 'Scotland Yard telephoned to say that Ketch would not repeat anything more, and that he appeared to be much better.

'At 9.35, Scotland Yard telephoned, to say that no one had been seen to enter or leave the Koestler Hotel since 6.30 the previous evening.'

'Odd,' interjected Dawlish. 'I think Bill had better get that place raided. Don't worry about the times, Yvonne, the gist of it will do fine.'

'I have it all here,' said Yvonne. 'Colonel Whitehead telephoned to find whether you were sleeping, and to ask Miss Deverall not to disturb you, but to say that the arrangements had been postponed for the day. Does that mean anything?'

Dawlish said: 'A lot, and it's worth hearing.'

Yvonne went on primly: 'The Middleton Nursing Home telephoned to say that Mr Beresford had passed a quiet night, and had recovered consciousness. He had asked the Matron to telephone the flat to say that he had seen and heard nothing, but had been attacked by a man entering the flat by the back door.'

'Bad luck,' said Dawlish, 'but thank heavens it's nothing worse. Next please.'

'Scotland Yard telephoned to say that the salvaged items from the fire at Drayton and Mattley revealed nothing in any suspicious.'

'They wouldn't,' said Dawlish. 'The damage was done. Anything more?'

'No. That's all.'

'We-ell,' said Dawlish judiciously, 'we can't grumble, I suppose. I would like to know where Bowing is, and whether he went willingly. Yvonne, when you accused Bowing of letting you down, did you mean it personally, or did you mean someone or other who worked with him?'

'It was someone there,' Yvonne said, 'it must have been.'

'What's all this about?' demanded Clay quickly.

'You'll learn,' said Dawlish, and was about to raise his cup to his lips when he stopped with it half-way, and said in a much sharper voice: 'What's this? No word of Andy?'

'Nothing at all,' said Felicity quietly. 'I've called his flat, and tried all his clubs. Then I thought the police had better look for him, so I told them he was missing.'

'I'm glad you did,' said Dawlish. 'My oath, is it another show like Beresford's?' He stared about him, and then added: 'Well, we have to take it. There should be some news of things in the post, soon.'

The telephone rang, and Dawlish lifted the receiver quietly, expecting it to be Trivett or Whitehead. But it was a different voice, one he knew, though now it whispered.

'*Captain Dawlish*,' whispered Bowing. 'I want *Captain Dawlish*. And hurry, I've got something very important to tell him.'

Dawlish said sharply: 'Dawlish speaking.'

'Oh, thank goodness!' exclaimed Bowing. 'I've managed to get away, but they're after me. Come to the cottage, come as soon as you can. You know, Course Cottage.' There was a pause, and then a sharper note in the youngster's voice. 'I can hear them in the passage, they're looking for me. Listen, it's worse than you thought, it's a lot worse. You mustn't be long, you've got to stop them from getting away from here!'

'It's all right,' said Dawlish. 'I'll be there. Try to dodge trouble—'

He stopped speaking, for there was a shout over the telephone, followed by a long drawn out gasp. The instrument clanged loudly, deafening Dawlish, although he strained his ears to catch the next sounds. He fancied he heard an oath, and Bowing's name. He thought he heard a scream. Then silence.

Within seconds Dawlish had rung up Whitehall, and while he held on looked round at Tim.

'Call Whitehead on the other 'phone, tell him that there's an attempt to get me down to Course Cottage, Woking, and that I'm getting the local police to surround the place. Ask him to send some men as well,' he said rapidly.

Tim leapt to his feet and disappeared without a word.

When Trivett came on the line Dawlish lost little time

explaining what he wanted. Trivett wasted none in asking ques-tions, but said crisply that he would fix it. By the time he had finished, Tim had stopped talking to Whitehead, who had agreed as promptly as Trivett.

'We-ell,' said Dawlish softly, 'either Bowing was lying and it was a put-up job, or else they had him prisoner there and he managed to escape. In either case, we're going.'

'Pat—' began Felicity.

'I know, darling, I know. But I promise I will take care. Tim, get your hat—Clay, are you coming?'

'I certainly am,' said Clay.

'Good man. Fel, hop along for the Bentley, will you?'

Felicity hurried out of the flat immediately, and the only one who kept silent was Yvonne. She stood by the window, looking out, as the three men leapt into the car, a set, strained expression on her face.

'He always *has* won through,' she said in a tight voice, 'hasn't he?'

'Ye-es,' said Felicity, 'but one day he might not.' She drew a sharp breath, then stood up quickly, saying that there was plenty of work to be done.

CHAPTER NINETEEN

COURSE COTTAGE AGAIN

'Well, well, well,' said Patrick Dawlish, as he turned the Bentley along a side-road leading across the golf-course near Woking. 'There it is, every brick in the right place!'

'You sound to me as if you were going on a day's outing, not to a ruddy show which might see the end of you,' said Tim. 'Last night I thought you were worried.'

'Last night I *was* worried,' said Dawlish. He pulled the car up outside the gates of the cottage, and sat back to look at it. He saw a house of fair size, attractive and well built. The grounds were well laid out, and in fairly good order.

'The police hide themselves pretty well, we have to say that,' he continued cheerfully.

'There are trees enough for cover,' said Tim flatly.

'You're in a dour mood,' declared Dawlish.

He could not explain why his own spirits had risen, there was no reason for it at all. He had no more information about the telephone call, and could not guess whether it had been genuine, or whether Bowing was in fact a victim. That he had been taken to the cottage, if the telephone call had been genuine, was a puzzling thing, for it must surely be known that the house was watched?

Tim declared roundly that he thought it was a trick to get them down there.

'And well it might be,' Dawlish assured him. 'But we can't say for sure until we look around, and if Bowing is in trouble and was brought here, we need to see the place.'

'They've had an hour to get away,' said Tim.

'The Woking police have had fifty-five minutes to get the place surrounded,' Dawlish countered. 'Don't pay too much attention to him, Clay, he's not always quite so gloomy as this.'

They walked slowly along the drive towards the house, keeping their eyes open for trouble. From the porch Dawlish looked about the golf-course. A little group of men and women were standing about one of the greens. The sun was shining with more than spring warmth, while a few clouds drifted sluggishly across the sky. In the distance there was the hum of an aeroplane engine, and from nearby came the *crack!* as a ball was driven squarely down the fairway. It pitched on the next green, and Dawlish said:

'Not bad, eh?'

'We have come to look at this house, haven't we?' asked Clay shortly.

'Oh, yes,' said Dawlish, 'but we also have to get the lie of the land before we start battering down the doors. Bunkers to the right of us, bunkers to the left of us and a few pine trees in between. Or are they fir? I can never tell the difference. The nearest bunker is about fifty yards from the house, a queer place to have a bunker, seeing that it's quite a long way from the fairway. Don't you think so?'

'I've seen bunkers in queerer places than that,' said Clay, while Tim eyed the big man with fresh interest, commenting:

'You're getting at something.'

'There's a way out of the cottage, and consequently it must also be a way in. It's obvious to me that a great deal of time and trouble and expense was devoted to planning this place. Do you happen to remember it being built, Clay?'

Clay said: 'I didn't see it, if that's what you mean, but I heard about it. My uncle didn't spare expense. He always spent freely when it was on a new house.'

Dawlish said: 'Oh, did he? Say that again.'

'Now look here,' began Clay, but when he saw the expression in Dawlish's eyes he stopped the protest, and repeated what he had said with an almost schoolboy preciseness.

'He always spent freely when it was a new house.'

'And how many new houses did your Uncle Thomas build?' Dawlish asked quietly.

'Oh, five or six. He was a bit of an invalid, and always moving from one part of the country to another. He could never find a house that he really liked, so he had one built to his own design. I don't suppose he's the only man with a foible like that.'

'Indeed, no,' said Dawlish. 'On the other hand, one could hardly call it a commonplace habit. How many of the houses have you seen?'

'Three,' said Clay, after a moment's pause.

'Are they all alike?'

'There isn't much difference,' admitted Clay.

'Just as quickly as we can, we want the addresses of those houses,' said Dawlish. 'And now let's concentrate on getting in here.'

He reached for the knocker and brought it down with some force.

The reverberations of sound faded, and there was no response. Dawlish pressed the bell, then knocked again, but had the same reward. It did not seem to worry him, and he stepped away from the door, a solid one of oak, and went to the nearest window. There he put his elbow through the glass, unexpectedly enough to make Clay exclaim in surprise.

'Part of the Dawlish service,' said the big man. 'Lots of policemen are looking this way and wishing they could stop me.' He unfastened the catch of the window, pushed it up and then climbed through.

When the others joined him, Dawlish had an automatic in his right hand.

'No reception party as yet,' he said, 'I rather thought there might be. Guns in hand, forward we go. Clay, you're new to this. Stand at the side of that door, nearest the hinge, and when you've turned the handle step back and push it open with your foot.'

'So you seriously expect trouble,' said Clay grimly.

They split up in the hall, searching the rooms quickly. But they were all empty; nor was there anyone upstairs. The windows were closed, and there was a faint mustiness in the air.

'Bowing was lying,' said Tim suddenly.

'We haven't finished yet,' said Dawlish. 'There's a cellar.' He led the way downstairs, and tried the handle of the door beneath the stairs. It did not budge, although he put all his weight against it. Scowling, he stepped back and considered it, knowing that it must be bolted on the other side, for the key turned freely in the lock.

'We could use some heavyweights on this,' he said. 'Tim, you and I will try together.'

They drew back while Clay stood by and watched in some surprise. Together they launched themselves against the door. At the second and third attempt they could hear the hinges groan, and the slow creak of splitting wood, but it took them five minutes more to get the door down.

Beyond them it was very dark.

Dawlish groped for the electric light switch, and a lamp at the foot of the stairs went on.

'I think we'd better have some help,' said Dawlish. 'Hop out and get some of the Roberts, Tim. You might see some of Whitehead's boys, too.'

Tim hurried off, while the others walked down the stairs, Dawlish telling Clay of the exit through the wall, and a little more of what had happened at his first visit.

By then they had reached the cellar. They found the outer room, where the play had been rehearsed, empty, and just as Dawlish had left it. He attempted to open the door leading from it to the second room, but it would not budge.

Footsteps sounded above their heads, heavy and deliberate. Tim came hurrying down the stairs with two policemen behind him. There were other Woking men upstairs, he said, and two or three of Whitehead's men were already in the grounds.

'Good,' said Dawlish. 'Now I wonder what's blocking that door?'

He opened the door from the stairs, but the room beyond was in darkness, and it was some seconds before he found the switch. His hand hovered over it for a second or two in an odd reluctance to press it down; then he told himself briskly not to be a fool. The light clicked on.

He blinked, then stiffened, while Clay exclaimed aloud.

Stretched on the floor was the body of a youth. The red hair made it horribly clear who it was, even before he saw the face. He knew that it was Bowing, and that he was dead.

Dawlish, Tim Jeremy and Clay returned to London an hour after their gruesome discovery; Dawlish to Whitehead's office, where he had arranged to meet Trivett. The Superintendent was there first, and Whitehead was talking quietly to him in his mellow, urbane voice.

The greeting of the three men was brief. 'You've heard about Bowing?'

'Yes.'

'I imagine that he was killed just after telephoning me,' said Dawlish. 'He hadn't been dead long.' He paused and then said woodenly: 'They had knocked him about quite a bit.' His face was set hard, and something of the scene at Course Cottage was brought vividly to the mind of the other man. 'There was no sign of anyone else,' Dawlish went on. 'The whole place was empty, as well as the subterranean tunnel which was used the other night for the acting party to leave. It leads to a bunker some distance from the house. I can tell you one thing; a lot of people had moved about in that bunker during the night. The top layer had been raked over to cover the tracks, but it wasn't well done.'

'They were?' asked Whitehead quietly.

'Bowing's killers,' said Dawlish. 'I should have found how they got out of the place, of course, I took too much for granted.'

'Go on,' said Whitehead.

'What they had there I don't know,' said Dawlish, 'but it must have been pretty well hidden, not to have been found when we searched the place yesterday. However, we've made some progress. We know that they wanted certain information from Bowing. We don't know whether they got it.'

'How do you work that out?' asked Trivett, speaking for the first time.

'Why torture him?' demanded Dawlish. 'They wouldn't waste the time just for the sake of it, knowing we'd be down post haste. He was keeping something to himself, and they got wind of it.

However, if Bowing can't talk Clay's son can. The uncle, owner of the house at the golf-course, had five other houses built on the same lines. It's possible they have the same cellar accommodation. I've a list of the addresses here,' he added, and pulled out his wallet. 'The Clay family was in this up to the neck.'

Trivett and Whitehead looked at the list.

There were houses at Hampstead, Cheltenham, Hunstanton, Ealing and Winchester, and in each case the name of the house was 'Course Cottage'. Clay had told him that all of them were built near golf-courses, golf being a game he was particularly fond of.

'He seems to have been particularly fond of a few other things also,' said Dawlish harshly. 'Will you get those places covered at once, Bill?'

'I'd better get over to the Yard now,' said Trivett.

He left the office immediately, and when he had gone Whitehead and Dawlish eyed each other in silence for a while, before Whitehead spoke. 'And your theory?'

'There's support for it now. Bowing rang through to say that the affair was worse than we had thought—which is the idea that occurred to me. He was killed to prevent him from talking, and I fancy that he was tortured to find out whether he knew anything of what was brewing, and had passed it on. Obviously he was taken prisoner and kept at Course Cottage, where he made a discovery of overriding importance. That's as far as we can go.'

'Ye-es,' said Whitehead. 'But it's all rather vague, Dawlish. I left a message for you that the removal of the internees has been postponed, but I don't know whether it will carry beyond today. You've certainly got the support of the Under-Secretary at the Home office there,' he added with a chuckle. 'It's about the only thing you've done which meets with the gentleman's approval.'

'So we've something under twenty-four hours,' said Dawlish. 'And the next camp on the list is Borlash—if they don't change the order of operations.'

'Are you going up there?'

'It might be an idea,' said Dawlish. 'Yes, I think I will. Tim and Clay can come with me.'

'I've wondered about young Clay,' said Whitehead quietly. 'Are you wise to take him about with you? He has had a nasty time, of course, and he probably feels that he wants to be in it, but—'

Dawlish said: 'I'd like to take him, sir.'

Whitehead smiled a little. 'And it's obvious that I mustn't ask you why! You'll go by air of course—you want me to arrange that, I suppose?'

'If you will,' said Dawlish a little stiffly.

He left the office a few minutes afterwards. He was worried, his good spirits of the earlier morning gone completely. That Bowing had made a discovery of importance, and that it widened the scope of what was happening was obvious. The trouble lay in whether he could find out how much wider the scope of the affair had become.

That there was little time, and that something pretty big was brewing, both worried and frightened him. It might be a deliberate attempt to cause fire at all key points in Government offices, it might be sabotage on an even greater scale. The use of the little green 'cards' would ensure fires in the most carefully guarded places. Cordite factories, for instance, anywhere where high-explosive was used.

'This is getting me down,' Dawlish confessed to the world at large as he turned into Audeley Street. 'But there's nothing beyond a possibility to get my teeth into, no cause for action. Until things start, and then it'll be too late.'

As he let himself into the flat he heard an announcer speaking over the radio. He entered the lounge, where Tim, Felicity, Yvonne and Clay were gathered. All of them were looking towards the radio, listening to the suave tones of the announcer:

'. . . anyone finding such cards should immediately report to the nearest police-station, first removing them by picking them up with the point of a pin, a knife or similar instrument. The cards are extremely inflammable, and should be taken to the nearest police-station, or waste ground, or wherever they can do least harm should they catch fire.'

'Well, well,' said Dawlish. 'Someone's got a move on. I wonder who managed to work that oracle?' He paused, and then added: 'But I wish I knew whether I'd do more good here or in Scotland.'

CHAPTER TWENTY

BORLASH

The setting of Borlash Camp was very different from that of Drayton or Mattley.

Dawlish, Clay and Tim saw it for the first time from the air, a little after five o'clock, when dusk was settling over the lesser highlands of Scotland. The tiny town of Borlash, on the banks of a narrow river, was a mile or more to the west of the camp, the wooden huts of which were camouflaged, and picked out with difficulty.

Along the road to the camp ran a valley between high hills, now shrouded in mist. As the 'plane flew lower, Dawlish could see the wire fence, manned by a guard even stronger than there had been at Mattley. What was more, he saw a number of small searchlight units and machine-gun posts.

The pilot said curiously: 'They weren't there yesterday.'

'Borlash means business,' said Dawlish quietly.

Colonel Pendexeter, the C.O., was a grey-haired, up right man who had been warned to expect the party. He greeted them affably enough, and without preamble, plunged into the details of the precautions he had taken. Ten searchlight batteries had been stationed about the camp so that at the first hint of trouble they could go into action.

'It'll make it easier for the guards, and our machine-gunners,' said Pendexeter. 'None of the internees can get out if we do it properly. And we will,' he added grimly. 'I'll make sure that none of the beggars escape from *this* camp.'

'I'm sure you will, sir,' said Dawlish perfunctorily. 'What precautions have you taken against an attack from outside?'

Pendexeter turned sharp grey eyes towards him.

'Outside? What do you mean?'

'At Mattley—' began Dawlish.

'Oh, there were a few people who helped the escape from the outside, yes,' said Pendexeter. 'We'll have machine-gun posts near and frequent enough to cover anything like that. And the passes and glens over the mountains are all covered.' He cleared his throat, and then added: 'You had me worried for a moment, I thought you expected a serious attack from outside.'

'It could happen,' said Dawlish.

'Now come, Captain Dawlish, we have to be reasonable. I have had the fullest instructions, and there is no indication that the trouble starts anywhere but inside the camp. Not that I think a great deal *can* start,' Pendexeter added, 'but I don't mean to take chances.'

'No-o,' said Dawlish. 'Nevertheless that is exactly what you are doing, sir. In all about a hundred and fifty male internees are at large, and it is just possible that they have found their way up here. You ought to be ready for trouble both ways, and quite serious trouble. From, say, armed guerrillas.'

'My dear sir!' exclaimed Pendexeter.

'I can't imagine a better place for the internees to hide,' persisted Dawlish. 'You've hills all around you.'

'The movement even of individual strangers would be

reported,' Pendexeter pointed out, 'even if the gossip of the crofters and villagers didn't very soon bruit it about. I can assure you that there's been no large-scale movement of strangers near *Borlash*, Captain Dawlish.'

'I can understand that, sir,' said Dawlish stubbornly, 'but I have to point out that we're working against unknown forces of whose strength we are as yet quite unaware. I'd like to feel that at least half of those batteries of searchlights, with their machine-gunners, were turned in the opposite direction. Or additional units brought up,' he added.

'You are serious, I suppose,' said Pendexeter slowly. 'There is nothing in my orders to hint at the necessity for such a suggestion.'

'I know,' said Dawlish, 'but I've come up here to try to make sure that we catch incomers as well as outgoers, sir. I can't support my request, but—'

'Oh, I'll see that something's done,' said Pendexeter grimly. 'If this thing doesn't fizzle out at Borlash, I'll—'

He broke off without completing the sentence, and gave orders into the telephone, crisp and businesslike. Dawlish, much heartened, followed him into the Mess where several of Pendexeter's junior officers were gathered.

He saw at once that Borlash had been well organized.

The equipment of each internee had been thoroughly examined, beds had been stripped, pictures taken down from the walls, libraries inspected, each book shaken to make sure nothing was hidden in it. The junior officers were obviously impressed by Pendexeter's thoroughness, but one of them said:

'I've never known the swabs so cocky, all the same.'

'You've mostly German-born folk here, haven't you?' asked Dawlish thoughtfully.

'They're all German-born,' he was assured, 'and with one

or two exceptions, the most unpleasant type. If they make any attempt to get out tonight many of our fellows will enjoy going for them.'

Darkness had now fallen over the camp, and there was a damp chilliness in the air. Pendexeter was here, there and everywhere, but at half-past seven he joined Dawlish and the others in the Mess.

'I've humoured you,' he said cheerfully. 'If by any chance you *are* right—and I can't allow that you are, you know!—everything has been done that can be done!'

'Those inflammable cards are easy to hide,' said Dawlish cautiously. 'I'd like to go outside, sir. Is that all right with you?'

'I'll join you shortly,' promised Pendexeter.

There was no moon, and the stars were hidden again: the three men who had flown from London were glad of their greatcoats. The sounds which came from various parts of the camp were muffled, and in the gloom there was no hint or suggestion of the hundreds of watching men. For an hour Dawlish moved around, trying to peer through the darkness, feeling a sense of depression, almost of frustration.

On the nine o'clock news there was a repetition of the warning to the general public about the little green cards, but no other news that Dawlish thought worth hearing. Alone, for the others preferred the Mess to the bleak night, he stood by the door with a sentry pacing up and down not far from him. No glimmer of light broke the darkness.

'Let's hope they won't try it,' he said aloud. He thought grimly of the arrangements being made to remove the prisoners. He wished that he could clarify his objections to such a move, but clung stubbornly to the belief that only by stopping an attack which actually took place, and taking prisoners from amongst outside agents, could they find where the internees were being taken. That was surely an essential thing. Trivett might arrange for the inspection of all the houses which Thomas Clay had had built to his own specification, but there was little likelihood that evidence of an incriminating nature would be found in them. Where were the escaped internees?

How were the 'cards' brought into the country? Or were they manufactured in England? That seemed the most likely thing.

When he contemplated that possibility, and the extent of the organization obviously engaged, he felt a helpless and almost savage anger that he had done nothing but arrive too late at every scene of action.

Quite suddenly, without the slightest warning, a flash of flame came from the direction of the huts.

Although he was looking for it, although he expected just that, it took him by surprise. He stared towards the flare, which dimmed for a moment, and then increased. Hardly had the flames started to streak upwards when he heard the wailing of the siren. The Mess door was flung open, Tim, Clay and Pendexeter tumbled out with half-a-dozen junior officers.

'So they're tryin' it, b'God,' snarled Pendexeter between his teeth, '*now* we'll see what's what.'

He dashed off towards the fire, but before he had gone a dozen yards other outbursts started at different huts. Suddenly the searchlights were turned on, great beams of light spreading a bright glow about the earth, showing up everything, even the fires, in unnatural prominence. Men were running towards their posts, and Dawlish, looking about him, saw that the search-lights were pointing away from the camp to make sure that no one approached from the mountains.

'What are we going to do?' Clay demanded sharply.

'Watch and wait,' said Dawlish. 'I'm going up on the roof. Give me a hand, Tim.'

But he needed little help as he hauled himself up to the flat-topped roof and then was joined by the others. They stared at the grotesque scene, the eerie light, showing up the machine-gun posts and the batteries. Dawlish, watching the main huts, saw the internees streaming out, heard a volley of shooting as the gunners fired over the heads of the crowd, in a desperate attempt to stem the rush. It had no effect. He saw the prisoners spreading out, running towards the wire fence.

The fence remained intact.

At Mattley he knew, the fence had been broken by fire and outside agents, the men he was counting upon finding, and suddenly he thought that the precautions he had urged had caused the men to stay away, leaving the internees to their fate. He felt a sickening sense of futility, until Tim shouted:

'A *tank*. Look at that!'

Dawlish peered in the direction of Tim's pointing finger, and saw a small tank careering across the open ground towards the fence. A dozen machine-gunners fired towards it, but did not stop its progress. It drew nearer the fence, and then crashed into it.

'It's got through!' gasped Tim.

'There's another,' said Clay in a high-pitched voice. 'And a third!'

The tanks—midget size and extremely mobile—were moving at great speed in three or four directions, crashing through the wire one after the other. They seemed unaffected by the shooting, while as they smashed down the fences waves of internees made for them. At first the confusion was so great that it was difficult to tell friend from enemy, but gradually Dawlish was able to pick them out.

He cried: 'Come on, Tim.'

They jumped from the mess roof, then piled into a stationary car, making for the nearest gap. A dozen internees came rushing towards them, but at a shot from Tim's automatic they drew back.

A tank had turned and was racing towards the mountains, its mission accomplished. It went at a good speed, unaffected by the volleys of machine-gun fire turned towards it, and Dawlish wondered whether there was a chance of catching up with it once it reached the rough ground of the foothills.

He drove doggedly on, determined that if it were humanly possible, he would do it. The tank he was following reached the road, by-passing a nest of machine-guns, then settled down to a high speed.

Dawlish, still vivid in the glare of the searchlights, raced the car for all he was worth. He was gaining, doing a full fifty miles an hour to the tank's forty. He thought exultantly:

'He can't get away now, we've got him!'

Almost as he formed the words, the tank stopped. Three men scrambled out, and hurried across the hillside. A machine-gun nest opened fire, but it was too far away to stop them.

'We'll walk,' said Dawlish abruptly.

The three men leapt from the car, then began a pursuit across damp and boggy land. In five minutes Dawlish realized the dangers of it, for he went down to his ankles and had a struggle to free himself from the grip of the slime. Tim and Clay turned to his assistance, but he managed to pull himself free without help. The men from the tank appeared to be more familiar with the ground. They twisted and turned but did not once appear to be in difficulties.

The glow from the searchlights was getting fainter, and the men were now barely visible. Tight-lipped, Dawlish led the way, trying to follow the trail which his quarry blazed.

The men were at least two hundred yards ahead, when one of

them pitched forward. Without the slightest compunction his companions left him, continuing their flight, and as Dawlish and the others drew up they saw that the unfortunate man was already waist deep in a bog. 'Not much chance,' said Dawlish, 'but you can try.'

Clay hesitated, but Tim went forward immediately, testing the ground as he advanced. It buried his foot almost immediately. He went down on his stomach, stretching out his arms. Dawlish went on.

He imagined that the two men from the tank expected him to fall into one of the bogs. They twisted and turned this way and that, always on solid ground. The temptation to cut across country and thus lessen the distance between him and his quarry was strong in Dawlish, but he fought against it, knowing that there could be disaster in such a move. The distance grew neither greater nor less, but he was breathing hard, the weight on his legs, as he pulled them from the sucking earth, almost unendurable. The light was growing dimmer, soon it would be impossible to see his quarry. He heard nothing, and finally stopped, for to go on was to invite death: in that darkness they might be waiting for him behind a rock, and in any case it was no longer possible for him to choose the path with any accuracy.

He hesitated for a moment, and turned round.

He could just discern Tim and Clay with a humped figure between them. So they had pulled the fellow out, and the chase had not been entirely fruitless. Cheered, Dawlish made his way, slowly and cautiously, back. He tested every step he made before going on, and sweated at the thought of the recklessness with which he had started the chase.

He was soon within the glare of the searchlights and he stopped quite still, watching. The sight which met his eyes was a macabre one.

There had been several machine-gun posts in the road, but none of them appeared to be in action. There were figures stretched out by the sides of the guns. A little nearer the camp, he located the rattle of machine-gun fire. He saw dozens of men and women, hurrying up the road, tank fire covering their escape.

His fear of a guerrilla band had proved only too true.

He saw how cleverly it had been done, and could see no way of preventing the escape of the majority of the internees. There must have been two hundred of them hurrying up the road, while the tanks, converted into pill-boxes, prevented troops from coming up.

The effort had succeeded in spite of all Pendexeter had done, but the question which Dawlish had asked of Trivett the previous night reared itself again.

'Where will the escaped internees *go*?'

He uttered the words aloud, standing alone in the eerie light, thirty or forty yards from Tim, Clay and the man they had rescued. Then he looked ahead of the straggling crowd, peering towards the distant sides of the mountains, too far away from the searchlights to be illuminated, and gave a sudden, sharp exclamation.

A green light had appeared between the road and the mountainside.

He could not understand it at first, but then he saw the internees clambering over the side of the road and down into the glen, making for that green glow.

Grim-faced Dawlish watched the strange, distorted figures.

Then he too moved towards the road.

The idea came to him, suddenly, that he might be taken for one of the internees. He was in civilian clothes, and could mix with them without difficulty if once he could pass the stretch of bog-land. There was a stiff climb to his left, and although it meant going farther away from the main party of the internees he chose to turn in that direction, and then began the steep climb to the road itself. Once or twice he dislodged boulders, and nearly fell with them as they rolled down the side of the valley, but he kept going.

He did not know how long it took him to reach the road, but he did know that for some time everything had been hidden from him. Then he topped the ridge he had been climbing, and stopped for a moment to recover his breath.

The green light, which had been reduced to only a faint glow, now shone clearly at the side of the mountain. He was no more than three hundred yards from the rise over which the internees were going. Most of them had disappeared, and he thought he heard a strange wailing and crying sound, but put it down to his imagination. But it was real enough, for it went on and on.

Then he reached a point on a level with the ridge over which the escaping people had gone. He could see everything clearly, for the mobile searchlight shone straight on the other side, giving a strong, white light.

Farther ahead the green light glowed as if drawing on the internees by some strange magnetic power.

Dawlish stopped quite still, staring towards a scene so dreadful and so full of horror that he felt his stomach turn, and his legs grow unsteady.

Once over the rise, the internees had to go down a sharp descent, too sharp to pull up at a short distance. Obviously they could not stop their headlong rush; as obviously they were filled with mortal terror.

He saw, too, the explanation of the screaming and the wailing.

Beyond that ridge and sharp descent there was a stretch of bog, now black with writhing figures, their faces showing white in the glare of the searchlight, their hands raised upwards, as if in supplication. It was from them the crying and screaming came, but it could not save them, nor could they save the others, who, reaching the top, were compelled by their own momentum to go downwards with an ever-increasing speed, into the quagmire to the death which awaited them.

CHAPTER TWENTY-ONE

HORROR IN THE GLEN

Dawlish felt an awful fascination as he watched the screaming people fall to their doom. He saw the green light, glowing and beckoning, realized that it was the signal they had been told to go towards, not knowing what there was between them and the light itself.

At last he turned away.

There was nothing he could do to help the internees, and for a while he could not think clearly. But as he regained the road his mind worked more freely, and he was able to consider the horror dispassionately. It answered one of the questions which had preoccupied him more than any other, but he derived little satisfaction from it.

Tim and Clay and their prisoner were waiting for him near the car. The prisoner was a little bullet-headed man, still suffering from the effects of shock. His clothes were covered with slime as were his hands and face, while Dawlish's companions looked little better.

None of them had been able to see what had happened.

Dawlish, set-faced, climbed into the car, and when the others had joined him, started for the camp. Three times in the short run they were stopped by guards, taking back to camp the few internees who had been recaptured. He thought grimly that they did not know, yet, what manner of fate they had missed.

He did not speak once on the journey.

The confusion at the camp had subsided, and everything seemed to be working in orderly fashion. Most of the fires were under control, although little remained of the wooden huts. Neither the Mess nor the Colonel's quarters had been affected, however.

Dawlish pulled up outside a hut in which he thought Pendexeter would most likely be. A sentry said that the Colonel was inside, but kept Dawlish and the others at the point of a bayonet until a subaltern came to identify them.

'All right,' he said to the sentry, and the bayonet was withdrawn. Together the four of them went into the office, where Pendexeter was sitting at his desk, his face pale and drawn, a telephone at hand. He was speaking as Dawlish entered.

'Yes, anywhere within a fifty miles radius. Watch particularly the coast-line . . . Yes . . . What's that?' He paused for a moment, looking up at Dawlish, who waited until the receiver was replaced before saying:

'I don't think there is any likelihood of more than a few stragglers being at large, sir.'

'What do you mean?' Pendexeter demanded. He looked at the party's dishevelled state, and then at the prisoner, and his eyes narrowed. 'Who is this man?'

'One of an enemy tank-crew,' said Dawlish. 'I don't know whether he knows much more than I do.'

He told them what had happened, then, and the grimness of his voice added to the macabre horror of the story. At first, it was clear, none of them could believe that it had happened, but before he had finished they were convinced. The horror of that wholesale slaughter, and of the fiendishness of the plan which had lured the internees towards the green light, believing that they were going to safety, left them silent for an appreciable time.

Then all of them stared towards the member of the tank-crew, and the man began to talk even before they asked a question.

Dawlish sat in Whitehead's office, as dawn was breaking.

It was the second day in succession that he had greeted the day there, but this time he looked less tired, although his face was finely drawn. He was alone but for Whitehead, the others had returned to the flat, and the prisoner was at Cannon Row, where Trivett was going through his story again.

Whitehead listened to the recital without comment, and towards the end Dawlish said:

'So we no longer have to ask ourselves where the poor devils go. Those at Borlash were lured into the bog, and if we look hard enough we'll find the bodies of those from Drayton and Mattley. There isn't much doubt about that.'

'But *why?*' asked Whitehead.

'Part of the bluff,' said Dawlish. 'We thought that they were creating havoc in the internees' camps for a bluff, and now we know it. They didn't think we would find out what happened at Borlash, and if the O.C. there hadn't been receptive of ideas we wouldn't know now. They're releasing the prisoners and then killing them, because they want us kept busy on that problem alone.'

'It looks like it,' said Whitehead slowly.

'It is,' said Dawlish. 'Part of the bluff—my oath, what swine they are! And there are other things, sir. I thought we had the worst of them when Ketch and his men were taken in, but

Ketch was a part of the diversion, not of the main plan. They've a few tanks, at least, and they must have fifty or sixty armed men. Borlash is a good place to keep them, they stand more chance of getting away in the mountains than they do down here. But I think Pendexeter will get most of them,' he added with satisfaction.

'What did the prisoner say?'

'He confirms what we know,' Dawlish told him. 'There is a small group of German agents, some of them near Borlash. They've had a few tanks assembled in the mountains from parts smuggled into the country from Germany. The tanks are old models, they've been there for years waiting for something just like this. They did the trick all right.'

'Does he know anything about the cards?'

'He says that he knows they're used,' said Dawlish, and drew his hand across his forehead. 'The fires at Borlash were started by cards inserted in the mattresses. They've been there for some time, but kept in the air-proof container until tonight. They were mostly received by post.'

'And he said nothing else?'

'Nothing of importance. I don't think he knows anything,' added Dawlish, 'he was just one of the crowd. But mark my word, something else is brewing, something Bowing got wind of.' He paused, and then asked: 'Who put out the radio warning, by the way?'

'The Prime Minister,' said Whitehead. 'He gave orders as soon as the cards were shown to him.' Whitehead smiled a little, but then grew sombre. 'You say there's nothing more we can do?'

'There are Clay's houses,' said Dawlish, 'but Trivett's handling those.'

'They've all been raided,' said Whitehead. 'They were found to be almost identical with the one at Woking; they were, of course, empty. Here's Trivett's report.'

'Thanks,' said Dawlish, and looked through a typewritten statement.

At four of the houses, though empty, there had been evidence of recent occupation. In the cellars there were benches, and the rooms had been turned into workshops. There was no indication of any of the goods being made there, no evidence at all that they were the little green cards. The report was factual and detailed. No opinion was expressed.

Except by Dawlish.

'They were making the cards at the houses, of course, but they got wind of it in time to clear out. They've another rendezvous somewhere, probably a store-shed, and they'll distribute from there. They—'

He stopped abruptly, his expression blank, almost wooden. It was difficult to realize the speed with which his mind was working, but Whitehead knew him well enough to guess that he had seen a new possibility, was thrusting aside all the inessentials and trying to reckon it at its true worth.

He had suggested guerrillas: and that was what the men in the mountains amounted to. He had called the internees' escapes a bluff, and certainly the evidence suggested that he was right. Looking at him, Whitehead felt a little uneasy, and began to probe the possibilities which had made Dawlish look as he was doing then.

'Ye-es,' said Dawlish at last, speaking very softly. 'Of course, a store-shed. A place where they keep the cards. And what do they do with them, Colonel? They send them to prison camps and other places, by post. Why shouldn't they send them to Government Departments by post? We've seen the little green cards, but supposing the other things that they're going to distribute widely *aren't* green? Supposing they aren't even cards? Supposing it's ordinary paper impregnated with the phosphorous-plus? A nice thought, and one to ponder.'

Whitehead said: '*My oath!*'

Dawlish went on, almost as if he were in a trance. 'Distribution. And the easiest way to distribute is by post. But if they're going to send these things out by the thousand no private house or small business would do, because, as suspicions increase, an over-large posting would be noticed.'

Again Whitehead said nothing, and after a pause Dawlish went on:

'The easiest way would be through an established mail-order house. Or a Government Department, one or the other. I wonder how Thomas Clay made his money? And how Sir Alfred made his? They wouldn't be retired businessmen, would they?'

He did not ask for permission but stretched out for the telephone, and he was talking to Trivett in a few seconds. 'What's that?' he asked, his voice brisk enough, though he, too, had been up all night. 'We-ell, I'm not sure, Pat, but I think Sir Alfred was in some kind of brokerage business. Thomas Clay was a company promoter, but he also had side-lines. If you'll hang on a moment I'll get the files.'

'I'll hold on,' said Dawlish.

As he waited he looked at Whitehead, and there was a glint in his eyes. Musingly, he said:

'The simple things nearly always work, don't they? We don't look for them until we've tried all the complications, but I should have woken up to that by now. Sir Alfred was a broker, and his brother a company promoter. Both occupations could necessitate long mailing lists. And there were other activities, too . . .' His voice grew louder. 'What's that, Bill?'

'I said "Are you there?"' repeated Trivett at the other end of the wire. 'I have the *dossiers* here, Pat. Sir Alfred was on the Stock Exchange, but retired just before the war to take up the

Government appointment. His brother was a partner in the same firm, and also managing director of several small financial companies. To wit, moneylending; all proper and above board of course.'

'Hum,' said Dawlish. 'Good reputations?'

'Excellent.'

'Not a murmur against them,' continued Dawlish. 'There wouldn't be. Where are the offices, Bill?'

'In Putney now,' said Trivett promptly. 'After the London blitz started, they lost their Leadenhall Street offices. What's on your mind?'

'The Clays and their company. What's the concern called?'

'There are half-a-dozen small companies, but the chief one is the Clay Investment Corporation, at May Hill, Putney.'

'Any other directors?'

'Young Adam Clay, but he had little to do with the business,' said Trivett, 'and—'

'Go on,' said Dawlish as the Yard man paused, but it was a moment before Trivett recovered from what was obviously a considerable surprise. Then he said:

'A gentleman called T. H. K. McFee, Pat. Your McFee, I suppose.'

'Of course,' said Dawlish gently, 'the McFee who was so dour a Scotsman, but who financed Bowing and the others to keep us looking in the wrong direction. Bill, that place at Putney has to be raided, and no one, not even your men, have to know where they're going. Get into a car, lead the way for half-a-dozen other car-loads and if you're wise, have the men armed. Drive yourself, and tell them to follow you.'

'What about you?' asked Trivett.

'I'll be there,' said Dawlish. 'Oh, yes, I'll be there!'

He replaced the receiver and beamed at Whitehead, his

expression so cherubic that the Colonel smiled. But he was not really amused, for after a moment he said:

'You could be wrong, Dawlish.'

'Of course I could,' said Dawlish, 'but I'll put every penny I have on a wager that I'm not.' He grinned happily. 'Trivett will be a quarter of an hour getting his band together, and I can have a cup of tea and a snack here, can't I?'

'Yes,' said Whitehead, leaning forward and pressing a bell-push, 'but it won't be much.'

'A sandwich will do nicely, thank you,' said Dawlish, with the politeness of a small boy. 'Now I think Tim had better follow me after a decent interval—say half an hour. He can bring Clay, of course. Would you mind telephoning him to that effect after I've gone? He won't like it if I leave him out in the cold, and I don't think Adam Clay will be happy about it, either.'

'He won't like this new turn,' said Whitehead.

'No.' Dawlish nodded understandingly. 'You know, sir,' he added, 'we were very slow indeed. I was so sure that we were being led up the garden path about Sir Alfred Clay that we paid too little attention to him. Then we swung round and gave him plenty of attention, but we didn't think of his business interests.'

'We didn't know he had any,' said Whitehead.

'Ah, but we should have done,' said Dawlish. 'It was dropped on us rather quickly, I'll agree, but we should have had a comprehensive view of it all by now. Parmitter didn't mention Clay's other interests in his report?'

'No-o,' said Whitehead slowly.

'A pity,' said Dawlish. 'I know we're all pulling together, sir, but between you and me I rather think Parmitter has let us down. He couldn't be a friend of the Clays, could he?'

Whitehead said very softly:

'I hope not, Dawlish. I'll see him very soon.'

'Good,' said Dawlish, and then paused as the man brought in a tray containing tea and sandwiches. He had not known how hungry and thirsty he had been until he finished his third cup of tea. Flicking away the last crumb he said thoughtfully:

'This show is full of surprises, of course, but I think we can guess what Bowing discovered. He was brought to the house, and found out that McFee was one of the enemy. Then he almost certainly connected McFee with Thomas Clay, and drew the necessary inference. Doesn't that answer most things?'

'It does,' said Whitehead.

'Subject to correction, of course,' said Dawlish. 'And now I'll have to be off. You wouldn't care to come?'

'I must stay here for reports,' said Whitehead, regretfully. 'I hope you're right, Dawlish, but—' he paused for a moment, and then added quietly: 'If you are, you know what you're going into, don't you?'

'Oh, yes,' said Dawlish. 'Fire and water, and all that kind of thing. If we get there and they're at home, they'll set the place ablaze to give themselves time to get out. Which reminds me, the Putney fire people ought to be warned at once of an impending outbreak. Will you look after it?'

'Yes,' said Whitehead, 'I will.'

He did not shake hands, but stood looking at the door for several minutes after Dawlish had gone out. Then he went to the window, watching the street until he saw the green Bentley go along Parliament Street, towards Victoria Street, and then on to Putney. Dawlish would be at May Hill within twenty minutes, and at the pace he was going would get there before Trivett and his men. He would want to do that, of course: he would feel that he should be the first to force entry, but Whitehead's concern was lest he was the last to get out.

Dawlish was not thinking of that, but of the possibility that the letters which he so feared had been posted the previous night.

CHAPTER TWENTY-TWO

FIRE BY POST

The offices of the Clay Investment Company were in a private house near Putney Hill, an old Georgian building mellowed by time and tended by a succession of careful owners. From its first and second floors there was a fine view over Wimbledon Common, and, in another direction the spire of Roehampton Church could be seen, sharply outlined against the sky. From a corner window it was possible to keep watch on the traffic coming along Putney Hill, while from a window on the other side, the service road leading to the backs of the premises in Grove Street could be kept under view.

All of these things had been considered when Mr Thomas Clay and his brother had selected the house for 'evacuation' purposes should serious bombing develop in London. It had developed, and they had moved, but the business of the Investment Company had by no means dwindled.

On the contrary, it had increased.

No longer concentrating on the small investors, it had widened its scope and was in constant touch with most of the large industrial combines in the country, many private companies and most Government offices and factories. Its mailing list, according to Mr T. H. K. McFee, who stood by the window overlooking Putney Hill about the time that Dawlish left Whitehead's office, was quite the most comprehensive in the country. Contemplating the long room in which he stood, he felt he had ample justification to do so with deep satisfaction.

In pigeon-holes along the walls were letters by the thousand. They were split up into sections covering different counties. Already stamped and addressed, it was a task which had taken a depleted staff some three days to accomplish. It was McFee's delight that none of the staff had the faintest idea of what they were doing, working conscientiously for him and the company, then back to their various homes and voluntary work on the Home Front. That thought aroused McFee's frequently dormant sense of humour.

The letters for the London and Home County districts would be posted that afternoon, those farther afield would be in the post within the next two hours.

McFee stepped away from the window and took a letter from a rack. He weighed it in his hands, and his dour face broke into a smile. It looked so innocent, but if he were foolish enough to tear one open, within a few minutes the house would be ablaze, and his chances of getting out slight indeed.

Since the plan was McFee's alone, he had some cause for satisfaction.

He was not seriously perturbed by the possibility of failure. True, the radio warning about the green 'cards' had given him a turn, for he had not expected action so promptly. But the green cards were not to be used in this wholesale despatch of fire by post: he had taken precautions against that, on instructions from Berlin. It was surprising how smoothly and easily the communications came through. At the beginning, he had been apprehensive lest the counter-espionage service in England proved quick to discover the links through Spain and, occasionally in urgent matters, through Ireland. The idea of putting the messages in plays was a good one, and he had developed it well. He considered that Berlin should be very pleased with him.

The scheme had nearly come to grief, he knew. Sir Alfred Clay had been weak and vacillating, and Thomas Clay difficult in many ways; but now they were both dead. His remaining partner in the work of espionage and sabotage on a scale which, he assured himself, had never yet been conceived, was both reliable, and safe, and certainly not suspected.

McFee, heavily bandaged about the face, for he had been severely burned at Woking, turned towards the door. It was surprisingly easy to hoodwink the police, and although once or twice he had been worried by Dawlish, he had reached the conclusion that the big man was not to be feared. A heavy-witted oaf, thought McFee, comfortably.

He went slowly upstairs.

Lying in a small, darkened room, were Playfair and May Larkin. When McFee switched on the light the girl shrank back, moaning piteously, but McFee did not glance towards her. She was bandaged just as she had been when she had been brought from the Woking Hospital, and had not been given attention since. He hoped, however, to be able to get a doctor to look after her, a man who would not report her whereabouts to the police. Bowing had been fond of the little chit, and might have told her more than McFee wanted her to know.

He was just a little apprehensive lest Bowing had talked too freely.

At the sound of the door opening Playfair reared up in bed muttering: 'Put out the light.' Not so heavily bandaged as May Larkin the old man stared at McFee, his expression unreadable.

'What's the matter?' asked McFee, 'is it hurting your eyes?'

'That poor child—' said Playfair, looking towards the girl. 'The light, please.'

'It won't hurt her,' said McFee roughly. He pulled up a chair and sat down, not knowing that Dawlish was at that moment on a level with Trivett's car, heading seven cars laden with Flying Squad men, all ready for action, and not a quarter of an hour's journey from the house. 'You ought to start looking after yourself, Playfair.'

'I am an old man,' said Playfair wearily. 'There is nothing that can be usefully done for me.'

'Now be sensible,' said McFee reasoningly. 'You can be useful to *me*, Playfair.'

'We will not discuss it,' said Playfair, and there was dignity in his manner, and a courage which expressed itself in the calmness of his words. 'In no circumstances will I be of further help to you, McFee. Unwittingly I have worked against my country, but—'

'You damned fool,' rasped McFee. 'What difference will it make to you? *Your* country—you make me sick!'

Playfair said quietly:

'I shall not help you further, whatever you do to me.'

'We'll see,' said McFee harshly. 'You'll come to change your mind, or—' he paused abruptly, and then said: 'What else did Bowing tell Dawlish?'

'I know nothing more than I have told you.'

'Sometimes I think I ought to have put you away a long time ago,' said McFee savagely. 'I get tired of talking to you.'

'And I get tired of discussing this ghastly affair with you,' said Playfair. 'To think that I believed you were with us, to think that I allowed myself to be so completely deceived!'

McFee said softly:

'It's going to happen tomorrow, Playfair, and it starts today. There won't be a Government building in the country that hasn't had a fire. Good work, eh?'

'If there were only just one thing I could do,' said Playfair helplessly, 'just one thing, I would be happier.'

'There's nothing,' said McFee. 'Your legs are tied down to that bed, and you can't move. I'll be back to deal with you when the letters have gone out.' He laughed. 'Once they're off the premises there won't be a thing to worry about.'

He left the room, as Dawlish, a few hundred yards ahead of Trivett, approached Putney Hill from the High Street.

McFee went back to the room where the letters were waiting. By then two of the staff had arrived and were busy on other circulars. McFee thought of the way they had tucked the previous ones into the envelopes, little dreaming of what would happen when they were opened. It was really so simple, there were no complications at all. One had only to open the envelope and take out the circular, and enough friction was caused to set the circular on fire, with an explosive action nearly as fierce as that of the little green cards.

McFee said:

'Seven thousand three hundred, yes. That's fairly comprehensive.'

'Yessir,' said a pale-faced clerk. 'We got all of them finished.'

'I know,' said McFee, 'I know. If we get the results there will be a special bonus for you.'

He looked at the rows of sealed envelopes again thoughtfully. 'What time does the first post go?'

'About 8.40, sir.'

'We'll have the long-distance letters put in the post-box, then, at half-past eight.'

'Very good, sir.'

McFee nodded, and glanced out of the window. Then he stiffened. He had caught a glimpse of a green Bentley with a big, fair-haired man at the wheel. For a moment he could not believe his eyes. His mouth formed a single word stiffly, awkwardly.

'*Daw*-lish!'

'Did you say something, sir?' asked the clerk.

'No, no,' said McFee, and turned abruptly. 'Get as many of the long-distance letters as you can to the post-box immediately. Immediately, understand that. And go out the back way.'

'The—the back way, sir?'

'You heard me!' roared McFee. 'The back way! I won't be here for a few hours; if anyone asks for me, tell them I'll be in tomorrow, do you understand? Tomorrow. Don't give them any information about me apart from that.'

'I—I see, sir.'

'And get those letters into the post-box!' shouted McFee. 'Don't stand there staring at me, get them in!'

The clerk hurried downstairs as McFee called aloud to a heavily built, hard-faced man, one of three he had ordered to watch the approaches to the house.

'I've given orders to have the letters posted immediately, but I don't trust the clerk. You know what will happen if he opens them. The whole place will be up in flames in a matter of minutes; none of us will get out alive.'

'Leave it to me,' the man said, and went heavily down the stairs, while McFee turned towards the other two. 'One of you stay by these stairs, the other by the back stairs. If anyone tries to come up from the floor below, put them away fast.'

The two men grunted, and McFee went hurriedly up to the next storey, where he had his own apartment. He could not understand how Dawlish had managed to get to the Putney house, it must be more than coincidence. Bowing must have sent word; curse the red-haired brat.

Perspiration broke out on McFee's forehead and the nape of his neck. He wiped it away and moved to a window. Dawlish's car could not be seen, nor, indeed, was there any other. It looked as if the big man were attempting this on his own, and if that were so it would be all right. He saw the clerk moving off with the letters.

Those letters: *if* Dawlish opened one . . .

'Kell will stop him,' McFee muttered; 'he'll have to stop him. But why wasn't I warned, how did this happen?' He stood staring out of the window, playing with the idea of climbing out of it and down into the grounds. That was a fool's thought. If he needed to get out he could go by the back door; Dawlish could not be in two places at once.

He wished he had more help on the premises. Would it be safe to send for it? It would take an hour or more for help to come, probably nearer two hours. Dawlish had to be sent away, convinced that there was nothing the matter with the letters and the Company. But—but his name was on the list of directors on the earlier letter-heading, probably Dawlish had obtained a copy of that—or the police had.

McFee began to feel, without admitting it, that he was not quite so clever as he had thought.

Meanwhile Pat Dawlish, who had passed a note from his car to Trivett's, and knew that Trivett's men would successfully conceal themselves, approached the square Georgian house thoughtfully.

There was a name-plate with the words:

THE CLAY INVESTMENT COMPANY LIMITED REGISTERED OFFICE

in the porch, and the door was ajar. He opened it, and saw several other doors, all of them marked—one '*Private*', another '*Inquiries*', a third '*Appointments Only*'.

Dawlish walked in. The place appeared, at first, to be empty, but when he reached the '*Appointments Only*' door he heard footsteps, and looked up to see a heavily built, fresh-coloured man walking down the stairs. About the man there was an air of respectability often connected with financial offices, and on his broad, flat face there was an expression of surprise.

'Good morning, sir,' he said. 'Can I help you?'

'I'd like to see Mr McFee,' said Dawlish.

'Mr McFee, sir?' The look of surprise increased. 'I'm afraid Mr McFee is no longer associated with the company. Mr Slesser, the managing director, isn't in at the moment, but if there is any way I can help you I'll be only too glad. My name is Kell.'

'Thanks,' said Dawlish briefly. 'But Mr McFee is here, you know.'

'I beg your pardon?'

'He was seen at the window not long ago,' said Dawlish amiably, lying without a blush and watching the other carefully. 'Perhaps he lives here.'

'I'm afraid there is some mistake, sir.'

'I don't think so,' said Dawlish, and put his hand to his coat pocket, taking out his wallet. He noted the wary expression on the other's face, as he drew out a card.

Kell stretched out his hand, took the card—and then found himself looking into the muzzle of Dawlish's gun, taken from a shoulder holster with a movement which had seemed so casual that nothing hostile could spring from it.

Kell stiffened.

'Now what's this?' His voice was harsher.

'Commonly called a stick-up,' said Dawlish. 'I want to see McFee. Where is he?'

'You're quite mistaken, sir. I hope that—'

Dawlish said sharply:

'Turn about.' He saw the man's eyes sharpen, imagined that the fellow was estimating the chances of snatching at the gun and deciding that they were not good enough. Kell turned, and Dawlish said: 'Lead the way into each room, I want to look round.'

'I shall send for the police the moment you have gone,' Kell assured him.

'Good idea, you do that.'

Kell led the way into the four downstairs offices. There was a slightly musty smell about each of the rooms, but the thing he was looking for, a pile of letters, was missing. Frowning thoughtfully Dawlish directed Kell to go into the hall, thinking that Trivett would follow unless he had results quite soon. He had asked Trivett for half an hour without interruption.

'Upstairs,' he said abruptly. Again the man hesitated, but then led the way upstairs.

Dawlish looked about him, but was unable to see the man watching from the second landing, one who had a gun by his side and could have fired then, to kill him. But McFee's orders were clear-cut: there was to be shooting only if Dawlish forced his way beyond the first floor.

'This looks like business,' said Dawlish. 'Into that room on the right, please.'

The man stepped forward slowly.

Dawlish caught a glimpse of letters stacked neatly in their pigeon-holes, for the door of the room was ajar. When he saw the rest of it, a room at least thirty feet long and fifteen across, with letters stacked from the floor to a point half-way to the ceiling, he drew a deep breath, mingling satisfaction with a note of caution.

He stepped to the nearest pigeon-hole, and took out an envelope. It was addressed to:

'The Assistant Controller,
Post Office Savings Bank,
Morecambe, Lancs.'

He took out another letter, addressed to another Government Department at Morecambe, then saw one for the Commanding Officer of a Services Training Establishment.

'What's in them?' asked Dawlish.

Kell drew a deep breath.

'This has gone far enough,' he said sharply. 'I insist—'

'You're hardly in a position to insist about anything,' Dawlish reminded him, 'nor am I in a mood for it.' He stepped to a pile of open circulars on a desk in one corner of the room. These were the circulars similar to the ones in the envelope. He glanced through one of them, seeing that it held no importance or significance, and that there was no reason in the world why it should be sent to the Controller of the Post Office Savings Bank.

'All very interesting,' said Dawlish. 'Now supposing I see what is actually inside the envelopes?'

He picked up one, and tossed it to Kell, saying:

'Open it, and hurry up.'

CHAPTER TWENTY-THREE

KELL REFUSES

To Dawlish it seemed that the man had been holding himself on a tight leash. He felt quite certain that he had discovered how the cards, or their equivalent, were to be sent round to various Government offices, and he had in mind the fact that the other 'cards' had always been safe enough for a short while, until exposed to the open air. He believed a similar system would work with these.

Kell drew back.

'Certainly not. That is company business.'

'I thought I'd already seen what was inside the envelopes,' said Dawlish. 'Open it.'

Kell said thinly: 'Now listen to me. This has gone too far. If my clerks were here I would have sent for the police a long time ago. Put that letter down, and get away with you. I'm not frightened by your gun, you dare not shoot.'

'Right,' said Dawlish pleasantly. He put his gun down on the desk near him, keeping it within a few inches of his hand, and then began to open the envelope.

Kell said sharply: 'Don't do that!'

'Well, well,' said Dawlish. 'So it mustn't be opened.' He looked at the man evenly for a moment, and then began to tear the top, moving very slowly. As he did so he saw Kell's hand go to his pocket. Dawlish dropped the envelope and snatched up his gun, as Kell drew an automatic from his pocket, fired—and missed. Dawlish leapt towards him, sending the man reeling back against the wall.

The bark of the shot echoed clearly about the room, followed by the thump of footsteps as a man started to descend the stairs. Dawlish went towards the door, keeping close to one side and kicking Kell's gun before him. He felt a rush of excitement and satisfaction, and then he saw the second man, who had been stationed on the next landing, coming down with the gun in his hand.

Dawlish fired at his legs, and had better luck than Kell. The man pitched forward, the gun flying from his hand. As he fell he struck his head heavily on the floor, and sprawled inert.

Dawlish said sharply: 'Where's McFee?'

'You'll never get him, you fool,' Kell sneered. 'You think you're mighty clever, but if you're not out of here in two minutes the whole place will be burned down!'

'And you and I with it.'

'You won't dare—'

'I'll dare what seems necessary,' said Dawlish calmly. 'I came to get this job finished, but I won't start until the police arrive.'

Kell said in a startled voice: 'Police?'

'Oh, they're on the way,' said Dawlish.

He heard footsteps downstairs then, some of them hurried, and knew that Trivett and his men had been alarmed by the sound of the shots. He was thinking of the letters and the possibility that they were all inflammable. He did not think the man in front of him was lying, he was prepared to believe that the place would go up. Yet those letters wanted examining, he had to see more of them.

Trivett came into the room with two plainclothes men. A look of relief crossed his face.

'So you're all right,' he said. 'I thought you'd taken a chance too many.'

'I'm not sure that I haven't,' said Dawlish, 'there's something about this show that I don't like. But I think McFee's here, and we'd better look at the upstairs rooms quickly. Did you see anyone outside?'

'A clerk carrying letters to the post,' said Trivett. 'He's downstairs.'

'Send a man down and make sure those letters are neither posted nor opened,' said Dawlish urgently. 'Hurry, Bill, it's deadly important.' He half-turned to one of Trivett's men, but the Superintendent gave the order quickly and the man hurried downstairs.

Trivett looked at Kell.

'Is this fellow and the man outside on the floor your full bag?'

'So far,' said Dawlish. 'Listen, Bill. This joker is afraid of the letters being opened, and the chances are that they'll go off if we're careless. They might fire the house in any case, so get most of your men off the premises, but tell them to keep fairly near. Leave this to me to handle.'

Trivett said: 'Don't be an ass. McKenzie, get most of the men out. Call for three volunteers to stay in the hall downstairs, and two more for the landing. Tell them it's dangerous. And take this man with you.' Trivett indicated Kell, and then turned to Dawlish. 'We'd better start, hadn't we? Is there anything else?'

Dawlish said quickly: 'You might get more volunteers to take those letters out of the house and put 'em in the garden.'

'Arrange that, McKenzie, will you?' Trivett called to the man who was going out with Kell.

For a moment they were in the long room alone together. Dawlish gave a reluctant smile.

'You asked for it,' he said. 'We may get away with something, but I don't like the way things are going.' He led the way up the stairs, gun in hand, but saw no one. He went into two rooms with Trivett on his heels.

The door of the fourth was locked.

'A plain, straightforward lock,' said Dawlish. I can manage it, I think.'

'Let me,' said Trivett.

He took a skeleton key from his pocket, inserted it in the lock and turned this way and that: the *click*! came quickly, and he opened the door.

Both of them were on edge as they stepped through into a darkened room, uncomfortably aware that a single false move would be fatal.

Trivett switched on the light.

A moaning sound came from one of two beds, and from the other a startled exclamation.

'Dawlish!' a man gasped. 'Dawlish! Thank God, thank God!'

Dawlish saw that it was Playfair, and saw, too, that his legs were strapped to the bed. His eyes were feverishly bright and two spots of colour burned on his cheeks.

'Dawlish, the letters, you must get the letters. They're being sent out all over the country. They'll cause terrible fires, you must get the letters!'

'We've got them,' said Dawlish.

'You've—got—them,' repeated Playfair wonderingly. 'Oh, it's so hard to believe. Dawlish, McFee is here, he is the man you want. You must get him. He is a German spy and head of a terrible organization. Get him, Dawlish, you must get him!'

'Easy, now,' said Dawlish. 'We'll look after McFee. Bill, can you get someone to take the girl downstairs?'

He looked towards the other bed as he spoke, not seeing that Trivett had already gone out, but he heard the Superintendent calling for one of his men. Very carefully, May Larkin was lifted from the bed, and carried downstairs.

Trivett assisted Playfair until another man came hurrying to take over, then with Dawlish he moved out to the landing, looking towards the stairs.

'McFee was here,' mused Dawlish. 'And we've had so little opposition. Strange, we ought to have had a lot more. Come on.'

Warily, they mounted the stairs.

There was no sound when they reached a much smaller landing, but along a narrow passage they saw a door close abruptly. Then as they started towards it the door opened again, and someone fired. Dawlish, pressed back against the wall, felt the wind of the shot pass his face. There was another shot, and he heard Trivett gasp.

Dawlish moved rapidly along the wall, firing towards the door, which closed again. He heard voices inside, then turned to see that Trivett's right arm was hanging useless by his side. He hesitated, thinking that the house might be fired already, although McFee and whoever was with him would not readily turn themselves into part of the funeral pyre. It was nerve-racking, worse than any experience he could remember.

He fired at the lock of the door.

One bullet was enough to make the door sag open; he caught a glimpse of a man standing by the window and the head and shoulders of another, who was half-way out. The man getting out was McFee.

Dawlish fired at his companion. The bullet struck him in the shoulder sending him toppling forward. He knocked against

McFee, who lost his grip on the window sill and uttered a single high-pitched shriek. Seconds later there was a thud from outside, sickening and heavy. The wounded man stood leaning against the window, his face twisted, his lips working.

Dawlish said: 'Is this place going to blow up?'

'I—dunno!'

'Is it mined?' rasped Dawlish. He felt a deep conviction that it was, yet the need for a complete search of it, for taking out all the records as he had done at Clay's flat, was imperative. A wave of exhaustion swept over him. He knew that Playfair had not talked wildly, when he said that there was a dangerous organization; he knew also that there would be others to fill McFee's place. Everything had to be smashed, not only this one well-conceived scheme.

Trivett, looking very pale, said:

'We'd better get down, Pat, and start emptying the place.'

Dawlish gripped the wounded man by his sound arm and marched him towards the door.

As they went down the stairs the feeling that he was walking over a live volcano increased, every second seeming to bring an eruption nearer. He was on the first floor landing, seeing two men coming out of the room with piles of letters in their arms, when he heard a shout from downstairs and then a woman's voice.

'Pat,' called Felicity. '*Pat!*'

'My oath!' exclaimed Dawlish. 'What's she doing here?' He jumped forward, pushing the man in front of him, seeing Felicity half-way up the stairs. 'Get out!' he shouted, 'get out of here!'

'Pat, Yvonne's run away, she's in it!'

'Get out of the house!' cried Dawlish. He reached her, leaving the man he was escorting to one of Trivett's men. He gripped

Felicity's arm and rushed her down the stairs, but she, oblivious to the danger, was intent on what she had to say. 'Whitehead telephoned Tim and Adam Clay to tell them where to come. Yvonne heard the message. She left a few seconds afterwards, I couldn't stop her—she locked Tim in the bedroom with Clay.'

'Yes,' said Dawlish, barely listening. They were in the garden, and although he looked apprehensively behind him the house remained quiet and undisturbed, except for Trivett's men who were going in and out, removing records from all the offices, to cases standing at the extreme edge of the garden.

'She had a gun,' said Felicity, her hair disarrayed, her voice breathless. 'She took it out of her bag and told me to stay where I was, and to stop the others from coming here. She said they mustn't come here, that it wouldn't be safe, it would go up like the Brittling Hotel. She admitted she was in it, she'd been working for McFee and watching Bowing and the others. She came this way, I heard her shout "Putney" to a taxi driver.'

'We-ell,' said Dawlish, 'if that's the case she won't be long getting here. What about Tim and Clay?'

'I've no doubt they're on their way by now, but I didn't wait for them. Pat, haven't you seen her?'

'Not yet,' said Dawlish, 'but I think this ruddy place is liable to go up at any minute. I don't think she was lying about that. So for heaven's sake put my mind at rest and go to the end of the street. You can wait there.'

'Pat, you're not—'

'We've got to get it emptied,' said Dawlish desperately; 'we must have the papers to look through. I won't be long, but I can't leave it all to Trivett's men.'

With a wave of the hand he left her.

The police were, by now, reinforced by firemen, and there were two engines waiting; the hoses were being run out, long and grey, making patterns about the garden. From somewhere the police had obtained wheelbarrows. Papers and books were being dumped into them through the windows and wheeled to the far end of the garden. It did not take long, but it seemed an age.

Dawlish dashed up the stairs. He found McFee's room, and in it a safe small enough for him to handle. He staggered with it towards the door. Sweating and gasping he hauled it down the first flight of stairs, but as he reached the landing he saw Tim Jeremy, an ugly bruise on his right cheek.

'Gimme—a hand,' gasped Dawlish.

Tim seized one end.

'Fel's told you, I suppose?'

Dawlish grunted.

'I had the shock of my life,' Tim went on, his voice more than a little aggrieved. 'I thought you were sure that she was all right.'

'So I was.'

'Hmm. Must have been one of your less brilliant hunches,' said Tim. 'I wonder what's in this darned thing, it weighs a ton.'

'T.N.T. probably,' said Dawlish. 'Where's Clay?'

'He was with me,' said Tim. 'He looked pretty sick, I think he's fallen for Yvonne.'

Dawlish began to speak, then stopped abruptly. He was looking towards the front hall, seeing Clay advancing towards the stairs, his face set and grim. Then through the doorway came Yvonne, running swiftly. Dawlish had not seen her jump from a taxi and rush through the gateway, clearing the hoses without difficulty, and even warding off a policeman who tried to stop her. Most of the men had their hands full, and could do little. Yvonne came through the front doorway, snatching an automatic from her handbag as she started to climb the stairs, only a few steps behind Clay.

She snapped: 'Put that down, Dawlish! Put it down!'

He was standing with both hands beneath the safe, and knew that if he dropped it it would do serious injury to Tim. Yet if he held on, she would shoot. Her eyes were wild; there was a glitter in them, an ugly twist to her lips that boded no good.

Clay turned on the stairs, as if dazedly.

'Yvonne—'

'Put that down, Dawlish!' cried Yvonne, 'and get out of here. Clay, get out of here, you haven't many minutes left, it will go up. Hurry, for heaven's sake hurry. Oh, *mon dieu.*'

By then policemen were coming towards her, but she stood with her back against the banisters, so that her gun covered the hall as well as Dawlish and Tim, who either had to drop the safe and try to overpower the girl, or go past and take the risk of being shot.

She said in a tense voice:

'Drop that! It must be destroyed!'

'I thought that was it,' said Dawlish. 'Towards her, Tim!'

Tim lunged towards her in spite of the weight of the safe, and she fired at Dawlish. She was no more than a yard away from him, but he ducked and avoided the bullet. As the shot rang out a policeman jumped up from the passage and lunged towards her. Another man put a hand through the banister rails and gripped her ankle. She fell.

Policemen picked up the kicking, screaming girl, and carried her out. White-faced and tight-lipped, Adam Clay stood watching. Dawlish, once on the level ground, said with a gasp:

'Run for it now, all of you, clear out of this shack.'

He and Tim reached the doorway still bearing the unwieldy safe. Together they carried it to the end of the garden. Straightening up Dawlish saw that the police and firemen were streaming out of the doomed house.

He stood gasping for breath.

Felicity and Clay approached him, but he still thought they were too near for safety.

'The farther away the better,' he muttered. 'Come on.'

He put an arm about her shoulders, and with Trivett and Clay went towards the gate. Policemen were keeping well back, but still the expected explosion did not come. By then there were no men in the grounds within thirty yards of the house itself.

And then, suddenly, a sheet of flame belched from a ground-floor window; a second and a third followed, and as they stared, the house in less than five seconds became a mass of flames, roaring and hissing, giving off palls of grey smoke, in a white heat so intense that even the firemen were forced to go back.

CHAPTER TWENTY-FOUR

IN PLACE OF MCFEE

'And so it's over,' said Felicity slowly.

'Is it?' said Dawlish, sitting back in an easy-chair at the flat. 'I'd feel more certain of that if I knew who was going to take McFee's place.'

'Does it matter all that much?'

'I have a tidy mind,' said Dawlish, a trifle smugly.

Some twenty-four hours had passed since the fire at Putney, and the complete gutting of the house. But by then it was proved that the raid had been successful, for the safe had been opened. In it was a record of McFee's orders from Berlin, and the way in which he had maintained communication. There was work for the Foreign Office there, and for the countere-spionage men who worked abroad. There was work, already being done, for Whitehead's men and for the police, for there were the names and addresses of McFee's various agents up and down the country, and there were full details of three other little bands, in mountainous districts, with small tanks assembled, and arms and ammunition in plenty for guerrilla warfare.

Dawlish, in spite of his earlier words, seemed fairly satisfied.

'On the whole, I suppose, we can't complain. The tanks and the other arms were stored there two years ago in readiness for the invasion which never took place.' He smiled a little ironically. 'And then it seems that someone in Berlin, or even in England, had the bright idea of using them to distract attention while we were prepared for a general attempt at sabotage by fire. And the internees were brought in with the same idea. Thorough blokes, the Germans.'

Felicity said: 'Have they found the escapees from the other camps?'

'Yes,' said Dawlish, 'and it's not pleasant hearing. Those from Mattley were taken to a cave near Cheddar Gorge. It was turned into a lethal chamber.'

Nobody spoke, and Dawlish went on: 'Those from Drayton were taken to a disused slate quarry filled with water, and drowned. *En masse,*' he added, his voice harsh and expressionless. 'The Tanton people went to a big house prepared for them, and it was set on fire. They were locked in.' He paused for a moment, before adding: 'So McFee and the Huns believed that their secret was safe, and worked accordingly.'

Clay drew a deep breath.

'And you think that there's someone we haven't found yet?'

'I'm sure of it,' said Dawlish, 'and I believe Yvonne could name him.' Again he paused, to add after a while: 'You might find it a consolation to know that neither your father or uncle knew what was happening as far as the internees were concerned, they believed that the freeing of the prisoners was the beginning and the end of it all. Don't ask me why they took German money for that job. They did, and it can't be helped. Their only motive was profit.'

Clay drew a deep breath.

'Don't rub it in,' he said.

Dawlish shrugged. 'They say it's each man's privilege to go to hell his own way, you're not responsible.' He shifted more comfortably in his chair. 'Then everything that Bowing told us was true, but unfortunately for him, poor devil, he did not know that McFee and Yvonne were on the other side. Playfair was given a play to rewrite. We thought that it was his notion, but actually it was McFee's. The play contained a hidden code, and copies were circulated pretty widely. We know what happened to Bowing, and why. We know that May Larkin, who'll get better by the way, was a victim, as he was. We know that Playfair, with his gift for writing dialogue, would have been very useful to McFee, who tried to keep him. Playfair is pretty good,' Dawlish added. 'I *think*.'

Tim started.

'Here, what's this? Not *Playfair*?'

'Someone else is in it,' insisted Dawlish. 'Someone who will replace McFee, and get together the remnants of the organization so that it will live to fight again. Remember, we've found practically everything, but we haven't discovered where those inflammable cards and letters were made, and until we do, they're a potential source of danger.' He shook his head. 'No, we haven't finished yet.'

'But—' began Tim.

'I know, I know. It's not our job any longer, but I'm not so sure,' said Dawlish. 'We know how the letters were to be sent out, we know what would have happened in Government Departments and factories up and down the country, how commercial and industrial life in the country would have been brought to a standstill.'

Felicity brushed back her hair.

'And it's still hidden somewhere? The secret of it, I mean?'

'Still hidden, and still usable,' said Dawlish.

'Then what are you doing about it?' demanded Clay.

'At the moment, nothing,' said Dawlish, 'because it's no use chasing round the country looking for the machine which makes it, or the formula. It might be anywhere. No, we've just one chance.'

'And that is?' asked Tim eagerly.

'Find the man who'll replace McFee. Yvonne knows, and if it's necessary to give her what we call third degree—'

'Has it got to come to that?' demanded Clay.

'Now look here,' said Dawlish, 'this business is as foul as it can be. Of course it will have to come to that—if she won't talk.'

Clay stirred restlessly in his chair.

'You can't be sure that she knows.'

'We can be sure that there's a reasonable chance,' said Dawlish.

'It's a filthy business,' said Clay violently. 'I don't see how you can bring yourself to do it.'

'I don't like it,' said Dawlish. He glanced at his watch. 'I've got to see her at Cannon Row with Trivett now,' he said. 'If she won't come across—'

He shrugged, and stood up.

As he was speaking, Yvonne Lejeune, *alias* Yvonne Dubonnet, was alone in a small cell at Cannon Row. Her face was deathly white, her eyes were feverish and red-rimmed, for she had not slept. She seemed to have been questioned every minute of the day. She had forced herself to say nothing, for Dawlish was right in that, she knew who McFee's successor was. She heard footsteps in the passage, and a constable appeared. He had a tray with food, sent in from a nearby restaurant, for Trivett believed that she might be persuaded to tell them what they wanted to know if harshness were mingled with kindliness. She looked at it disinterestedly and pecked at it a little, but when the jailer entered to take the tray away the food had been barely touched. Then Trivett visited her.

He looked tired, but his face was set, and there was no sympathy in his voice when he spoke.

'You remember the man Ketch, don't you?'

'Well?' said Yvonne.

'And the way Dawlish handled him.'

She said nothing.

'If you don't tell Dawlish and I everything you know, you're going with Dawlish immediately,' said Trivett. 'He won't let up. You'll have to talk sooner or later.'

'I won't talk,' she said dully.

Trivett tried to persuade her but then left, knowing that Dawlish was due in a quarter of an hour. She might think better of it in that brief spell. He told the jailer to watch her, and the man, obeying to the letter, did not look away from her for a moment.

He told the story afterwards with an air of incredulous bewilderment.

He saw Yvonne put a hand to the lapel of her coat, and rub it between her fingers. It was an ordinary enough gesture.

'Just as if she'd been rubbing Aladdin's lamp, sir,' he told Trivett. 'One minute she was standing there, an' then—why, she just turned to fire. I've never seen anything like it!'

'I have,' Trivett told him sombrely.

That was after he had telephoned Dawlish to report what had happened, and when part of the police-station had been destroyed by the ensuing conflagration. There were no other victims, but Yvonne's body was charred beyond recognition.

Dawlish, hearing the story from Trivett, returned to the flat later in the afternoon, heavy-eyed and thoughtful. Much of it did not bear thinking about, and he looked very glum as he sat down in his easy-chair, facing Clay, Tim and Felicity. Then he repeated the story as the jailer had told it to Trivett, in a low-pitched, monotonous voice. Felicity could take no more, and slipped out of the room, while Tim stared at him, fascinated, and Clay sat with his cheeks a deathly pallor and his lips working.

Dawlish finished: 'And so that leaves, as suspects, only Playfair and May Larkin.'

Clay said thinly: 'Why the devil did you have to tell us in such horrifying detail? Isn't it bad enough to know what happened to her?'

Dawlish said quietly: 'The telling was necessary, Clay, I wanted you in the right mood.'

Clay stared at him.

'The right mood for what?'

'What I've been leading up to for some time past,' said Dawlish. 'Listen to another story, Clay, of a man who came into this affair and, when he heard my name mentioned immediately after his father's murder, rushed to see me instead of doing all the usual things. He—'

Clay said: 'You must be mad! What on earth do you mean?'

Dawlish went on imperturbably: 'Later he told me, this same adopted son, of an uncle's fine collection of houses, a collection which looked suspicious. The telling suggested that the son was on the square. But before those places could be raided, and it was done in an hour or two, our birds had flown. Had they been warned beforehand, Clay? I think they had.'

Clay said tensely: 'This is nonsense, I told you all in good faith. I've had nothing to do with it.'

'Haven't you?' asked Dawlish. 'Isn't it strange that when you and Yvonne met here you seemed to know one another, you were always saying and doing little things which made it likely that you were old acquaintances. And then she thought your name was in the safe. She didn't realize that you had removed it. She was prepared to give her life to prevent you being implicated, and to prevent us from finding where the inflammables are made. She did give her life, but she was wrong; she shouldn't have taken the trouble. We had you before, Clay.'

'You haven't a scrap of evidence!' snapped Clay, but his face was very pale and there was a glitter in his eyes.

'No?' asked Dawlish. 'Look at the things I've told you and see if they don't make evidence. Remember, you're the *only* surviving partner in the Clay Investment Company, remember that there had to be someone left. Listen to me, Clay. There isn't a chance of you getting out of it. Yvonne killed herself, she burned herself alive. Dying, she cried out your name. Yours, Adam Clay! And she didn't realize either that Playfair heard what McFee said to you when he last saw you, at Course Cottage, before the final getaway. McFee gave you away, Bowing tried to tell me, and Playfair has remembered that. And through it all, Clay, Yvonne's calling out your name. Do you hear her crying: "*Adam, Adam, help me, Adam!*"'

'No,' gasped Clay. 'No, it isn't true, you're trying to stampede me. I know nothing about it, I tell you!'

'You drove her to that, Clay, you drove her into it. Every moment she endured that horror is on your conscience. *Yours, Clay!*'

And then Clay sprang at him, snatching at an automatic in his pocket. But he did not draw it before Tim Jeremy stretched forward, and buffeted him aside.

Dawlish was sitting once again opposite to Whitehead, with Trivett at his side.

'Of course I bluffed him,' he was saying, 'and I don't think there was a tittle of real evidence against him, yet everything pointed his way. I couldn't bear to think that he would be detained under 18B and nothing worse, so I played on the Yvonne theme, as I've told you. Not nice, but are any of these things?'

Whitehead said slowly:

'You're right about that, but it was fine work. Clay's flat has been searched, and the formula and everything we need was there. The papers and cards were manufactured at the various "Course Cottages". There isn't anything left to worry about, and I hardly need to say "congratulations".'

'Great Scott, no!' exclaimed Dawlish. 'I was late most of the time. However, it worked out. And Ted Beresford is sitting up and taking nourishment, I'm told, while Andy Cunningham's turned up, thanks be, and will be all right after a week or two's rest. We can't complain.'

'I'm not complaining,' said Whitehead, 'and I don't know of anyone who is likely to. What about Playfair?' he added, 'and Bowing's girl?'

'Doing reasonably well,' said Dawlish. 'We'll have to get them fixed up in decent jobs. You can arrange it, can't you? May Larkin and poor Bowing—they were fond of each other; it's been a grim business. And the oddest thing is that if they'd put Bowing and the others out immediately they grew suspicious, we might not have been brought in. They tried too many diversions. They shouldn't have let us get on to Clay.'

'I've never really seen why they did,' admitted Trivett.

Dawlish smiled at him.

'Bill, that's your trouble, you have the direct mind and these shows work on the same principle as an onion, a skin within a skin. Still, they thought we'd be satisfied with having Sir Alfred and getting the internees' trouble settled. And so we nearly were.' Dawlish heaved himself from his chair, ambled to the door and then raised a hand in valediction. 'Now I'm going away for a week, and Felicity is coming with me. Don't write to us,' he added imploringly, 'we shall probably both jump a mile if we see a letter on our tray.'

ABOUT THE AUTHOR

John Creasey, born in 1908, was a paramount English crime and science fiction writer who used myriad pseudonyms for more than six hundred novels. He founded the UK Crime Writers' Association in 1953. In 1962, his book *Gideon's Fire* received the Edgar Award for Best Novel from the Mystery Writers of America. Many of the characters featured in Creasey's titles became popular, including George Gideon of Scotland Yard, who was the basis for a subsequent television series and film. Creasey died in Salisbury, UK, in 1973.

THE PATRICK DAWLISH MYSTERIES

FROM OPEN ROAD MEDIA

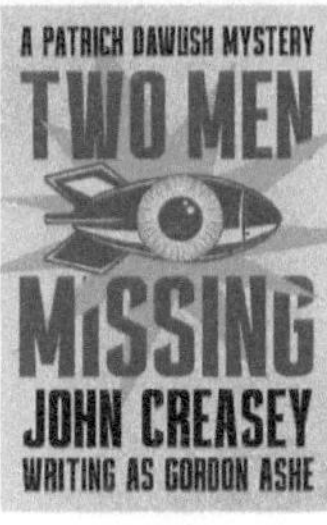

EARLY BIRD BOOKS
FRESH DEALS, DELIVERED DAILY

Love to read?
Love great sales?

Get fantastic deals on
bestselling ebooks delivered
to your inbox every day!

Sign up today at
earlybirdbooks.com/book

www.ingramcontent.com/pod-product-compliance
Lightning Source LLC
Chambersburg PA
CBHW050316110726
47899CB00007B/2269